The Hardy Boys
in
The Mystery of the Spiral Bridge

This Armada book belongs to:

_____

_____

_____

The Hardy Boys Mystery Stories

The Mystery of the Spiral Bridge

Franklin W. Dixon

Armada

First published in the U.K. in 1972 by
William Collins Sons & Co.. Ltd., London and Glasgow.
First published in Armada in 1974 by
Fontana Paperbacks, 14 St. James's Place,
London SW1A 1PS

This impression 1978

Printed in Great Britain by
Love & Malcomson Ltd., Brighton Road,
Redhill, Surrey.

CONTENTS

The huge bear lunged from the cave

·1·

Bad News

"CHECKMATE!" said Frank Hardy, as he glanced across the chessboard at his brother Joe.

"Okay. You've got me." Joe frowned at his trapped king. "I can't keep my mind on the game, waiting for that call and wondering how Dad is."

Dark-haired Frank, eighteen, and blond Joe, a year younger, sat in their laboratory next to a short-wave radio set. The room, filled with the latest scientific and detecting apparatus, was located over the garage behind the Hardy home in Bayport. Suddenly a metallic voice filled the lab. Both boys became tense.

"Radley calling Frank and Joe! Do you read me?"

"Roger," replied Joe. "Where are you, Sam?"

"Fifty miles from Bayport. We ran into a storm which slowed us down. Jack Wayne is preparing to land. Incidentally, boys, we've been tailed all the way from Kentucky! The other plane keeps just far enough away so that we can't identify it."

Frank pushed closer to the microphone. "How's Dad?"

"Sorry. No change."

"We'll have an ambulance waiting," said Frank.

"Roger. Over and out."

Immediately, Frank phoned Dr Bates, the family

physician, who had already been notified that Fenton Hardy was gravely ill. The doctor promised to arrange for the ambulance to meet the plane.

The brothers had hastened downstairs and entered the house by the rear door. The boys' mother and their aunt, Gertrude Hardy, were waiting anxiously in the living-room.

"Dad's arriving shortly," Joe announced. "Come on. We'll all drive to the airport."

The four Hardys hurried to the family car and Frank took the wheel. For a while they rode in silence, oblivious of the pleasant air, reflecting on the near tragedy which had overtaken Fenton Hardy.

Once a famous detective on the New York City police force, Mr Hardy now had his own successful investigating practice. He had often been assisted on cases by his sons, who had gained renown for their talent as amateur sleuths. Sam Radley was Mr Hardy's able assistant, and Jack Wayne was his private pilot and close friend.

Laura Hardy spoke up. "I had a strong feeling this case would prove unusually dangerous when Fenton agreed to accept it."

Mr Hardy's assignment had been to investigate suspected sabotage on part of a road being built by the Prito Construction Company in the Kentucky wilderness. Mr Prito was the father of one of the Hardy brothers' best friends, Tony.

A bridge on which the construction crew were working had collapsed. The county inspector was accusing the firm of having used faulty material, although this had been ruled out by tests. However, Mr Prito had discovered that bolts had been removed from supporting steel girders. Inquiries among the workers had shed no light on the identity of the saboteurs

The detective had flown to Kentucky in his personal plane, piloted by Jack Wayne. But the day after his arrival Mr Hardy had mysteriously disappeared. Sam Radley had already been summoned to help on the case and was to have met his boss for a briefing at the construction site that same day.

When Mr Hardy did not appear, Sam had gone to the neighbouring small town of Boonton, sure that the investigator would soon return. But Fenton Hardy was gone for almost a week.

His family recalled vividly Sam's account of the detective finally stumbling into Boonton, his hands manacled behind his back, gravely ill and delirious. The small local hospital had diagnosed pneumonia, but with baffling complications, and urged that he be returned home immediately.

Sam had reported, too, that no clue had been found to explain who had held Mr Hardy prisoner, or where. Also, his briefcase was missing.

As Frank swung into the parking area of the airport, Joe leaned excitedly out the window.

"There's Dad's plane. Jack's bringing her in!"

Minutes later the family stood near the ambulance, waiting alongside the apron. The four watched the blue-and-white, single-engine plane glide to a landing and taxi up to the ambulance.

Two white-coated attendants hopped out of the ambulance and joined Frank and Joe as they rushed to the craft. The cabin door opened. Sam Radley poked his head out. "Your dad's already on a stretcher," he told the boys.

They leaped aboard. Both gasped at first view of their father. A rugged man, Fenton Hardy's face normally had a healthy glow. Today he looked pale and drawn, and his eyes were closed. Gently the brothers and Sam lowered the stretcher to the attendants.

Laura Hardy wept softly as her husband was carried towards the ambulance, and Aunt Gertrude tried hard to hold back her own tears.

Joe bent over the stretcher. "Dad, can you hear me?" Mr Hardy's eyelids fluttered. His lips moved feebly, but no intelligible words came out.

"Still delirious," said Radley. "He's been mumbling like this on and off. I couldn't catch a thing."

"If only we could get a few words," Frank said. "They might give us a clue to the fiends who did this to Dad."

The stretcher was placed in the ambulance. The Hardys and Sam looked back at the plane. Jack Wayne, sombre-faced, peered out of the cockpit and waved. Then the pilot taxied the craft to its hangar.

It was decided that Frank and Mrs Hardy would accompany the patient, while Aunt Gertrude, Joe and Sam would go in the car. Soon the ambulance was speeding towards Bayport.

Joe, at the wheel of the Hardy car, asked Radley, "I didn't notice any plane landing before we left the airfield. You have any idea who was tailing you?"

"No. The guy was clever—kept a safe distance all the way."

Joe looked troubled. He was thinking hard. "Sam, I have an idea," he said. "I'll go home for our tape recorder. We can set it up by Dad's bed in the hospital, just in case he says something understandable when we're not there. We need a clue desperately."

"It's worth a try. Maybe we'll get some answers to vital questions in this mystery. For instance, who masterminded your father's kidnapping? Where was he held? And how did he get back to Boonton, handcuffed and sick the way he was? Somebody must have brought him there, but why?"

"We'll get to the bottom of this!" Joe vowed. He turned off the highway and headed for the Hardy residence at the corner of Elm Street and High Street. Aunt Gertrude, usually critical of her nephews' detective work, for once agreed.

"Oh, I'd like to get a hold of those—those terrible creatures myself!" she declared vehemently. "But please, Joe, you and Frank be very careful. We don't want you in the hospital, too."

"By the way," Sam asked, as they pulled into the driveway, "have you heard from my wife?"

"Yes," Joe answered. "She phoned yesterday, asking about you. She's fine."

Sam and his wife lived in an apartment near the centre of town, about half a mile from the Hardys.

Joe hurried to get the tape recorder. He tested it and put on a new tape. He and Sam were about to leave, when a taxi screeched to a stop in front of the house. To their amazement, Frank leaped out and rushed inside.

"Hey, what happened?" Joe greeted him.

"A clue, our first one!" his brother announced. He reached into a pocket, pulled out an envelope, and held it open to reveal a white, gritty substance.

"Where'd you find this?" Joe asked quickly.

"In the turn-ups of Dad's trousers. Come on. We'll examine this stuff right away."

The boys and Sam ran up the stairway to the lab. First the Hardys studied the white grains under a microscope. "Looks like tiny bits of rock," Frank observed.

"This could be limestone," Joe said. "Let's run a chemical test."

As Sam looked on, Frank shook the particles into a flask while Joe filled a beaker with clear limewater, then connected the two containers with glass tubing. Frank next picked up a bottle of dilute hydrochloric acid and poured it on to the grains. Bubbles appeared in the beaker and the limewater turned cloudy, then clear again.

"Limestone it is!" Joe exclaimed. "Sam, do you know of any limestone quarries around where you and Dad were in Kentucky?"

"Not offhand. But there are plenty of unusual rock formations. In fact, plans are under way for developing an immense park—sort of tourist attraction—featuring the peculiar formations."

"Near the highway construction site?" Frank asked. "Quite near."

As the Hardys put away the apparatus, the extension phone rang. Frank answered. "Hello. . . . . What was that? . . . I can't understand you. . . . Wait a minute." He turned to Sam. "Sounds like your wife, but she's awfully upset."

Sam grabbed the phone. "Hello? . . . Ethel?" A frightened look came into his eyes. "I'll be right over. Try to keep calm!"

He wheeled about to face the boys. "Something's happened to my wife. Let's hurry!"

The three pounded downstairs. While Joe sped into

"This could be limestone," Joe said

the house to pick up the tape recorder, Frank and Sam ran to the car.

"Aunt Gertrude!" Frank exclaimed, "We have to rush over to Sam's. Something's wrong. Wait here at the house, and don't let anybody in until we return!"

Miss Hardy got out of the car. "Very well. But what about Mr Kenfield? He's coming to inspect the roof today."

"Okay. But he probably won't have to come into the house. He'll use a ladder to get to the roof."

The Hardys and Sam sped to the Radley apartment. It was located on the first floor. The door was slightly ajar and Radley burst in, the boys at his heels. "Good grief!" Sam cried out.

His wife was lying on the living-room floor, her feet bound together and her hands secured in front of her with stout twine.

"Sam! Sam!" she sobbed. "Oh, I'm so glad you're here!"

Frank whipped out his pen-knife and cut the bonds. Mrs Radley, still trembling with fright, was helped to her feet. Joe hastened to get her a glass of water, while Sam insisted she rest in an easy chair. When Mrs Radley had regained her composure, she told them what happened.

"I'd been out shopping for about an hour. When I returned, I was surprised to find our door unlocked, but I thought I'd absentmindedly left the catch off. I went inside and almost fainted when I saw a strange man in the living-room."

The intruder had clapped a hand over her mouth, bound her, and warned her to make no outcry.

Frank wondered whether the prowler had anything

to do with the Hardys' case. "What did he look like?" Frank asked.

"He was tall, dark and—Oh, I can't tell you any more! I was so frightened."

"He was here for a purpose, that's sure," Sam said as he inspected the door lock. "It's been jimmied."

Nothing seemed to be disturbed in the living-room. Then the Hardys accompanied Sam into his study. One drawer of a filing cabinet was partly opened. Radley quickly examined the contents. "None of these files is missing," he said, perplexed.

Frank pointed to the top drawer. "How about that card index?"

Sam pulled out the drawer. "You're right! There are a couple of the cards sticking up, as if someone had riffled through them."

With painstaking care, the three sleuths checked the cross index of a long list of criminals which Sam had catalogued.

"You know there's a duplicate set in your dad's office," he told the boys.

By this time they had reached the names listed under M. "Mander—Manning—Matlack. Wait!" said Sam. "I'm missing the run-down card on Milo Matlack."

"Who's Matlack?"

Radley gave a low whistle. "He's an ex-convict, a dangerous character—one of the worst!"

· 2 ·

A Midnight Alarm

"IF Matlack's the bird we want, we'll clip his wings," said Joe, "no matter how tough he is!"

"Let's not jump to conclusions," cautioned Frank.

Sam went through the rest of the file. No other card was missing.

"We'll check the duplicate file right after we visit Dad," Frank said.

Satisfied that Mrs Radley was feeling all right, the Hardys left the couple. "We'll keep in touch with you about developments, Sam," Frank promised.

The boys hastened outside to their car and soon reached the hospital's parking lot.

"I hope Dad is better," Joe murmured, as they took the lift to the third floor. But he and Frank found Mr Hardy's condition the same. Mrs Hardy was quietly talking with Dr Bates. Both were looking gravely at the detective, who was breathing irregularly and still in delirium.

Noting Frank's and Joe's alarmed expressions, the doctor assured them everything was under control. "Your dad is very ill, of course. The pneumonia we can treat, but we'll have to conduct further tests to determine the exact cause of his prolonged loss of memory."

"How did he ever catch pneumonia?" asked Joe, stepping close to the bedside and looking down at his father's face, now flushed with fever.

"Possibly through extreme mistreatment," the doctor said. "Mr Hardy might have been kept in a dark, damp place without food and sufficient water."

Frank set his jaw grimly. "Could've been an underground prison," he declared, "which might explain the limestone in Dad's turn-ups."

Just then Mr Hardy turned his head on the pillow. His eyes were still closed. He mumbled, but as before, the words were still unintelligible.

Mrs Hardy sighed. "He's been doing that all the time I've been here," she told her sons.

Joe placed the tape recorder on the night table next to his father's bed, and explained what he had in mind. Frank plugged in the machine. Just then a pleasant-looking nurse came into the room. She introduced herself as Miss Tice.

"I'll be on night duty here," she said. "Is there anything special you'd like me to do?"

"Yes please." Frank showed her how to turn off the recorder and change the tape. He left a spare reel on the table.

"When you put on a new tape," Frank went on, "please put the used one in the drawer so that it won't be damaged."

The boys and their mother were assured by the doctor that Mr Hardy would respond to treatment.

"Your husband needs complete rest, Mrs Hardy," the physician added. "If there should be any change, we'll call you immediately."

Joe switched on the recorder, then the three Hardys

left the hospital and drove home. They found Aunt Gertrude setting the table for supper and gave her the latest report on her brother's condition.

"See anybody prowling around while we were gone?" Joe asked.

"Goodness no!" Miss Hardy said tartly. "Didn't we have enough worry for one day?" Then she added, "Mr Kenfield was here, of course. I heard his ladder being propped against the side of the house, and I saw his van parked in front."

Frank only half heard his aunt's words. His memory was suddenly jogged by another thought. "Joe! Let's check Dad's files!"

Aunt Gertrude fixed her nephews with a stern gaze. "Don't be late for supper!" she ordered. "We're having lamb stew and I don't want it to get cold!"

"Aunty," Joe said, "we're never late for lamb stew."

He winked at his brother and followed him upstairs to Mr Hardy's study on the first floor. From a secret compartment under a desk drawer, Frank withdrew the key to his father's extensive files.

Quickly they began looking through the cross index and the individual run-down cards.

"Nothing's been touched so far," Joe observed as Frank deftly separated the cards.

"Yes, everything's okay through L," Frank said, then started on the M's.

A moment later Joe exclaimed, "Hey! There's no card for Milo Matlack."

Frank grinned. "Don't get excited. Dad took the card himself and left this memo."

A slip of paper with Mr Hardy's handwriting bore the notation that the detective had taken not only the card, but also the complete dossier on the ex-convict with him to Kentucky.

"I knew it!" Joe burst out. "Matlack's our man beyond a shadow of doubt."

"Guess you're right," Frank conceded. "So, *if* we can find Milo Matlack, we may crack this case. Something tells me it'll be no cinch."

As Frank locked the files, Joe grabbed the telephone and dialled Radley's number. Sam answered. Joe first inquired about Mrs Radley.

"She's feeling better. But no leads yet to the intruder."

"Sam, we're hot on a trail!" Joe told Radley of Mr Hardy's memo, then asked if Sam could describe Matlack and give some of the criminal's history.

"I can't recall much detail," Radley replied. "But I do remember that Milo has grey hair."

"Where are we likely to find him?"

"Possibly in New York City, his old home."

"Then that's where we'll go!" Joe declared. Sam promised to round up all the information he could on the former jailbird. Joe thanked him and hung up.

"Boys! Supper!" Miss Hardy called.

The boys quickly washed, then hurried to the dining-room. Joe held a chair for his mother, and Frank helped Aunt Gertrude place a steaming tureen of stew on the table. As Mrs Hardy served, her sons told the women about the latest exciting developments in their father's mystery.

"There are two things Joe and I have to do!" said Frank. "Capture Milo Matlack and make him pay for what he did to Dad, and second, unearth the real story behind the bridge collapse."

"The police should handle such a—a fiend," Aunt Gertrude stated.

"The police can help us," Joe said, "but we want to collar Matlack ourselves."

Although fearful for her sons' safety, Mrs Hardy was proud of their courage and ability. Quietly she advised them to exercise the utmost caution.

"Don't worry, Mother," said Frank "We will."

After supper the boys went to their father's study and discussed the mystery until bedtime. Before retiring, Frank telephoned the hospital and learned that Mr Hardy's condition was about the same.

Late that night the boys were jolted from a deep sleep by the shrill jangling of the telephone. Frank switched on the bedside lamp and dashed to pick up the hall extension. Joe followed.

The caller was Miss Tice, the night nurse. "You're to come right over to the hospital," she told Frank in a tense voice.

Frank's heart sank. "You mean the whole family?"

"Certainly not," replied the nurse. "Just you and your brother."

"We'll be there," said Frank and hung up. Hurry, Joe! Something must have happened!"

Hastily the boys changed from pyjamas to street clothes.

They were grimly silent as they whizzed through the the streets to the hospital. They took the lift to the third floor. It seemed forever until they reached it and the door slid open. The boys rushed to the nurses' office.

"Is Dad—Fenton Hardy's condition worse?" Frank asked the nurse in charge. "Is that why Nurse Tice called?"

"Mercy, no!" she whispered. "If anything, your father is slightly improved."

Although relieved, Joe said wryly, "We sure had the daylights scared out of us!"

"I'm afraid we've had the daylights scared out of us, too," the nurse replied. "Miss Tice will explain."

On tiptoe, Frank and Joe ran down the corridor. Nurse Tice, red-faced and distraught, met them outside Mr Hardy's room.

"Why didn't you post a guard here if you expected trouble?" she asked indignantly.

Frank gulped. "Trouble? Did someone try to hurt Dad?"

"No, not that."

"Tell us what did happen!" Joe said impatiently.

"A man, dressed as an intern, sneaked into your father's room, that's what!" said the nurse.

Frank drew a deep breath. "And then?"

"I was coming back after my coffee break," Miss Tice continued, "and I saw this man in white removing the tape from the recorder. I was so surprised I cried out and he came rushing at me. I tried to stop him, but he got away." The nurse looked puzzled. "Why anybody would steal a tape with just mumbling on it is a mystery to me!"

·3·

Who is Felix?

FRANK and Joe stared at each other in dismay. "We should have had someone guarding Dad," Frank said glumly.

"Well, there are two police officers here now," Nurse Tice replied.

"Policemen?" queried Joe. "Where?"

"They're searching the building. The night supervisor phoned headquarters as soon as I reported seeing that thief."

The Hardy boys had hoped to handle this case mostly by themselves. Now the police had already been called in. Sensing there concern, Miss Tice became apologetic. "I don't usually flare up like that," she said. "But it was an unnerving experience."

"We're sorry you had such a scare," said Joe. "I'd sure like to get my hands on that phoney."

"At least," Miss Tice said, "you still have the tape."

"What?" Frank exclaimed. "I thought the thief got away with it."

"I forgot to mention I'd changed the tape." The nurse opened the night-table drawer and pulled out the first tape.

"Thanks a million," Joe said. "We'll take the recorder and play the tape when we get home."

When the nurse had checked Mr Hardy's pulse and

respiration, Frank asked if she could describe the thief.

"The man was tall," she said, "with jet-black hair and a moustache." The imposter, she added, had worn a mask which she had almost torn off during her tussle with him. "If I'd known judo," added Miss Tice, "I might have caught him!"

The boys exchanged glances. Except for the moustache, this description resembled that of the intruder at Radley's apartment!

At the sound of brisk footsteps in the corridor, the nurse and the Hardys left the room. Outside, they met Chief Ezra Collig of the Bayport Police Department, followed by a patrolman, who held a rumpled white jacket in his hands.

"Hello, Frank, Joe," the husky, keen-eyed chief said. Collig was an old friend of the Hardy detectives. "When I learned your father was here, I wanted to investigate this matter myself."

Joe looked at the jacket. "Is that the one the thief wore?"

"Yes," replied the chief. "We found it near the ground-floor fire exit." Collig's eyes narrowed. "Are you sure, Miss Tice, there was nothing else stolen from this room? Like hypodermic syringes or sedatives?"

"Positive the nurse assured him."

Frank spoke up. "Joe and I hope to solve this mystery on our own, Chief, but we'd like to brief you on it."

The boys gave the officer a concise account, ending with their plan for possibly picking up a clue on tape.

"Good idea," the chief said. "I'll do my best to help you. At least we can have an alert sent out for anyone resembling the intruder. I'm posting a guard on this floor, and also will have this jacket analysed in our lab."

"Thanks, Chief. That's swell," said Frank.

When the police had gone, Frank asked the nurse, "Did you have much of a tussle with the thief?"

"No. When I grabbed his mask, he pushed me aside and ran."

"Would you mind showing me your finger-nails?" Frank requested.

The woman held out her hands. Using a pocket torch, Frank carefully scrutinized both hands. Suddenly he said, "Here's something—a wisp of black hair!" He pointed to the nurse's right forefinger.

"Why, I never noticed it!" she exclaimed.

Miss Tice removed the tiny hair, which Frank folded in a sheet of white paper and put in his slacks pocket.

The young sleuths took the recorder, thanked the nurse for her co-operation, and left the room. Outside Mr Hardy's door was a patrolman whom the boys knew. He assured them, "No sneak thief will get by Tim Callahan."

"The Hardys grinned. "I believe it," said Joe.

As soon as they arrived home, Frank and Joe went directly to their lab. Frank was first to study the strand of hair under a microscope. "Joe! Take a look!"

His brother did so. "Say! That hair's grey near the roots. It's dyed black!" Joe was exuberant. "Matlack's for sure. I bet the moustache is phoney too."

Both boys were exhilarated by the thrill of their discovery. Now for the tape. Did it, too, hold a valuable clue?

Soon the tape was revolving on the machine, and although Frank had turned the volume up full, there were great stretches of silence. These were interspersed by Mr Hardy's mumbling, which was indecipherable—

except one word that came through with relative clarity.

"What's that, Joe? Something like 'licks'? I'll play it back." The strange word, or part of a word, came over three times.

Joe listened intently. "Sounds to me like Felix," he said.

"Could be. Perhaps Felix is a henchman of Matlack's." Frank shut off the machine and Joe telephoned police headquarters. Chief Collig was still there.

"Chief," said Joe, "do you know of any underworld character named Felix? We think that's a word which came over on the tape."

Collig said this did not ring a bell, but he would check his files thoroughly. "I'll let you know."

When Frank and Joe returned to the house, they quietly went to the kitchen and made cocoa. As they drank, the brothers discussed the night's events. Suddenly Joe put down his cup. "Frank! In all the excitement we forgot to check the airport for the plane that tailed Jack!"

Frank immediately telephoned Bayport Airport, and learned that one other plane from Kentucky, an air taxi out of Louisville, had asked for landing permission the previous afternoon. It had taken off a short while ago.

"Joe, that Kentucky pilot must have been the one who tailed Dad's plane!" Frank exclaimed. "Wish we could've nabbed him."

"Where is he headed?" Joe asked.

"Kennedy Airport in New York."

Because it was too late for the Hardy boys to do anything further, they tumbled into bed. Early the next morning Aunt Gertrude summoned them to breakfast. Although the bacon and scrambled eggs were delicious, Frank and Joe hardly tasted the food. Directly after the meal, the boys rushed to the telephone in their father's study.

It seemed an interminable wait, but Frank finally contacted an official at Kennedy. The man said that an air taxi from Louisville had landed early that morning and discharged its only passenger.

"Is the plane still there?" asked Frank.

"Yes," was the reply. "The pilot is checking weather reports. Would you like to speak with him?"

Frank's eyes brightened. "Certainly would!"

The pilot, who proved to be an accredited flier, reported that his passenger, a dark-haired, tall man with a moustache, had carried a large roll of hundred-dollar bills, from which he had peeled the fee for the chartered flight.

Upon hearing that he had flown a suspected criminal, the pilot whistled. "I wondered why he seemed so nervous about the plane ahead. Kept telling me not to get too close—just an act, I guess."

Frank then asked, "Do you happen to know where he was heading?"

"Afraid not. Just that he was going to take a taxi into the city."

Frank thanked the flier and hung up. When he told Joe what had happened, his brother said, "Well, at least, if the rat's in New York City, maybe he won't be pestering Dad."

The boys went downstairs. Suddenly they heard a series of loud bangs from outside. Aunt Gertrude ran out of the kitchen with a startled squeak. But her nephews only grinned. They recognized the source of the noise.

"That's only Chet's jalopy, backfiring," Joe said.

This conclusion was verified by a cheerful whistle as Chet Morton came through the back door. Frank and Joe entered the kitchen just as Chet, their best pal, plopped his ample frame into a chair. A longing look came over his round, freckled face.

"Oh—oh," Joe said knowingly. "Guess who's ready for a second breakfast?"

Chet was known far and wide for his never-failing huge appetite. "We-ll, I could use a snack."

"Humph!" Aunt Gertrude sniffed. "After you scared us half to death with that noisy jalopy?"

"That backfire is getting better, isn't it?" Chet said good-naturedly.

Soon he was enjoying a thick bacon-and-egg sandwich on toast and a glass of milk, served by Miss Hardy.

"Sure is a beautiful day, fellows," he said, between bites. "What say we take a ride on Barmet Bay in your motorboat?"

"Not a chance," said Frank.

"Why not? By the way, have you heard from your father?"

The brothers related everything that had happened. Chet was shocked to hear of Mr Hardy's illness. "Boy! He must have run into a gang of dangerous criminals."

Joe could not resist saying, "In fact, that hospital prowler might turn up around our neighbourhood."

Chet swallowed hard. "W-what? Are—are you going after him?"

"Sure thing," Frank said. "You want to help us?"

Chet groaned. "Count me out! This is vacation, remember?"

Fond of fun, opposed to hard work, and inclined to

back away from danger, Chet nonetheless was staunchly loyal to his pals. When necessary, he pitched in with two-fisted determination to assist Frank and Joe in threatening situations.

Now the chubby boy looked up sheepily from his second glass of milk. "You know, if you really need me, I'll—"

"That's the spirit!" Joe grinned. "We'll expect you to come on the run if we call for help."

"I'll be available."

Excusing themselves, Frank and Joe once more hastened to the study. First they checked with Chief Collig. There were no clues on the intern's jacket, and no Felix in the police files. Then Joe phoned Sam Radley and listened with raised eyebrows as the operative talked.

"Sam, you've really been busy! I'll take that down." Joe wrote quickly on a note pad. When he hung up the phone, he told his brother, "Sam contacted a New York prison where Matlack served time. He was released a year ago, and went to live in New York with a widowed sister. I have her address."

"What a break!" Frank exclaimed. "All clues point to Manhattan—so that's our next stop."

He called Jack Wayne, who agreed to fly the boys to Kennedy early that afternoon. When the brothers announced their plan, Aunt Gertrude objected. "You can't just leave us," she said. "I know the police are protecting your father, but what about your mother and me?"

"I can help," Chet offered.

"Great!" said Frank. "Mabye Biff, Tony, and Phil can, too. We'll call them for a meeting."

Within an hour the three boys had joined Frank, Joe, and Chet in Mr Hardy's study. Biff Hooper was a well-built six-footer whose favourite pastime was boxing. Tony Prito, slightly shorter, was handsome with an olive complexion and dark eyes. Phil Cohen, slender and agile, had an easy-going manner. His friends admired his great talent for drawing and painting.

"I sure feel terrible about what happened to your dad," said Tony. "Especially since he was working on this case for my father. Tell us what to do."

Frank and Joe outlined their plans. All four of the Hardys' chums would take turns helping Radley guard their home, and if necessary, relieve Collig's guards at the hospital.

"I hope you nail this guy Matlack," said Biff. "Good luck!"

After lunch and a visit to see their father, Frank and Joe drove to the airport. They left their car in the parking lot and hurried to meet Jack at the plane. Twenty minutes later the boys were looking down on the green countryside five thousand feet below, as Jack headed for New York.

The brothers were licenced pilots, and took turns at the wheel. But as they neared the metropolis, Wayne resumed control, contacted Kennedy tower for instructions, and soon brought the plane in.

Grabbing their suitcases, the Hardys thanked Jack for the lift and hopped out.

"So long," called the lean young pilot. "Call me if you need me."

"Will do!" The brothers hurried through the terminal, hailed a taxi, and headed directly for the address which Radley had given them. Presently they reached a dingy section of downtown Manhattan, and soon pulled up in front of a dilapidated building.

"This is it, Number 47," said Frank. He paid the driver and the boys got out.

The Hardys stood for a few minutes, noting the various details of the structure—windows, doorway, and fire escape. "Shall we make enquiries now?" asked Joe.

"Not yet. We better find a place to stay. There's a hotel down the street. Doesn't look like much, but at least it's close."

The young sleuths sauntered to the shabby hotel and mounted a short flight of steps which led into the dimly lighted lobby.

The brothers grimaced at the stale musty odour which greeted them. They registered at the desk and were given a key to Room 306.

"Cash and carry," said the clerk, a prune-faced individual with thinning hair. "Pay now and carry your own bags."

"Great welcome," Joe whispered wryly, as they climbed the creaking stairway.

Frank and Joe's room was no more than they expected: peeling wallpaper, one bare ceiling light bulb a sagging bed, and two lumpy chairs.

They had just finished unpacking when they heard the low growl of a siren outside. The Hardys looked out the window. Parked directly below was a police car, its red light flashing.

"Wonder what's up," Joe said.

The next instant the door to their room was kicked open with an earsplitting slam!

·4·

Attack From Above

STARTLED, Frank and Joe wheeled about to see a dark-suited man standing in the doorway, pointing a revolver in their direction. "Stand where you are!" he barked.

"Who are you?" Joe blurted.

"Detective Mulvey, New York Police Department."

Immediately two uniformed policemen stepped from behind Mulvey. "Turn round and put your hands high against the wall!" The brothers did as they were told and the police searched them. "They're clean," one said.

"What's this all about?" Frank protested. "We're not crooks."

"Identify yourselves." Frank and Joe pulled out their wallets and produced the necessary cards.

"Our father is Fenton Hardy," Frank said. "He used to work for the New York Police Department."

"I've heard of him. Good cop," said Mulvey. Then he apologized for the mistake. "But we have to follow up every tip we get."

"Tip?" Joe asked.

Detective Mulvey said a man had telephoned the police, saying that two dangerous criminals had registered in Room 306 at the hotel.

"Somebody sure has a tail on us," Joe commented.

"Who do you suppose he could be, Frank?"

"Beats me."

The detective spoke up. "Whoever it is, you obviously have an enemy. This is a rough neighbourhood. I advise you to return to Bayport."

"We've got to find a man named Milo Matlack," Joe said. "Do you know of anybody in this neighbourhood by that name?"

The three officers, who had just recently been assigned to the area, shook their heads. "But that doesn't mean a thing," said the detective. "A lot of the characters around here use aliases."

After the police left, Frank and Joe flopped down in the decrepit, overstuffed chairs, half angry, half amused.

"What a joke!" Joe burst out. "We're trying to catch an ex-con and we almost get nabbed instead. I feel as if I'm in left field without a glove."

"At least we've been alerted," Frank said. "We'll be on our guard every second."

After supper in a nearby restaurant the Hardys decided to turn in early. "Tomorrow we'll investigate that house first thing," said Frank.

As a precaution against prowlers the boys stood guard in four-hour shifts. The night passed uneventfully, however.

After an early breakfast, the boys walked to No. 47. They climbed the steps and rang the rusted bell. Several minutes went by. Finally the door opened just enough to disclose a woman in a faded pink housecoat peering out over the safety chain.

Frank introduced himself and Joe. "We'd like to talk to you about Milo Matlack, please."

"Milton who?"

"Milo—Milo Matlack. He lives here with his sister."

"Never heard of him." The woman's eyes, close-set in her pudgy face, regarded the Hardys blankly. She brushed her straggling hair back from her forehead. "You boys got the wrong place. Ain't nobody with that name lives here, and I know all my tenants."

"But *did* Mr Matlack live here at one time?" Joe said, growing impatient.

"Maybe yes, maybe no." The woman was about to close the door when a sudden noise from above made Joe glance up.

"Frank, look out!" he cried out. A metal dustbin was hurtling down towards the boys. They leaped aside, but the bin grazed Frank's shoulder, clattered on the steps, and rolled down to the pavement.

"Let us in!" Joe demanded. "Someone on your roof is trying to kill us!"

The safety chain clicked open. The Hardys dashed past the startled woman and ran up four flights of stairs to the roof. They glanced about in all directions.

"Over there." Frank pointed.

The small, monkey-like figure of a man was poised on the roof edge. He gave a flying leap and landed nimbly atop the next building.

"After him!" Joe urged.

Frank and Joe had to spring with all their might to equal the monkey man's leap across the five-story-high chasm. In doing so, they both sprawled on the tar roof of the adjacent building. By the time the boys had pulled themselves up, the small man had slithered down the fire escape and jumped to the ground.

Long before Frank and Joe had descended the iron ladder, their quarry was out of sight.

"Great horned toads!" said Frank, rubbing his bruised shoulder. "Who was that nut?"

"Just somebody trying to knock us off," Joe said angrily, and the boys hastened back to pursue their inquiry. The landlady now stood at the bottom of the front steps, having retrieved the dustbin.

"You hurt?" she asked Frank.

He nudged Joe, then replied, "I hope not, ma'am. But that was a close call. I could've been killed."

"You won't sue me or nothin'?" the woman said, wringing her fat hands.

As if debating with himself, Frank did not reply. The woman grew more nervous by the second. Joe now looked her squarely in the eye.

"We won't make any trouble for you, if you tell us about Matlack."

"Oh, all right," she said, unhappily beckoning the boys closer. "I don't want nobody to hear what I'm tellin' you," she whispered. "And don't you say I told you."

After Frank and Joe had promised not to betray her confidence, the woman admitted that Matlack and his sister had lived there. "They're gone now," she added gesturing with her hands. "I can't tell you nothin' more."

"Okay," Frank said. "Thanks."

The boys walked slowly down the street, conjecturing about the strange actions of the monkey man.

"I bet he's in cahoots with Matlack," said Joe.

"It's possible. Say, now that we know Matlack lived here," Frank went on, "let's question some of the other people in the street."

"Okay."

They entered what seemed to be primarily a hardware store, but which also contained a jumble of miscellaneous articles.

"Boy, what a junk shop!" Joe murmured, as they approached the short squat, man behind the counter. He peered gravely at the Hardys through thick-lensed glasses.

"We're looking for a man named Matlack," Frank said. "We understand he used to live in this neighbourhood. Do you know anything about him?"

The stout man stared unblinkingly at the Hardys, first at Frank, then at Joe, as if sizing them up. Then, suddenly, he broke into raucous laughter.

"Can't you answer our question?" asked Joe, annoyed.

The man stopped laughing. "Are you kiddin'?" he said gruffly. "If you guys don't want to buy nothin', get out!"

He stalked to the back and disappeared through a doorway. The Hardys shrugged and left.

Joe grumbled, "He must have had raw meat for breakfast!"

The boys continued down the street. Both were so engrossed in their quest that they were unaware that two tough-looking youths were trailing them, until one roughly elbowed Frank.

"Move over!" he snarled. "You own the whole street?"

"Excuse us," Frank said calmly.

"Oh, excuse us," the youth echoed mockingly. "Hey, Spike! A couple of real polite country boys!"

Joe turned on the pair, but his brother restrained

him. "Come on, Joe. Let's not waste our time. These two are spoiling for trouble."

The Hardys started on, but the second tough clamped a hand on Joe's shoulder, spinning him round. This was too much for Joe. He seized his assailant, and with a flying mare sent him over his shoulder. The fellow landed on his back with a grunt. His pal, meanwhile, had tried to grapple with Frank, but his success was no greater. Frank applied a half nelson, until beads of sweat stood out on his opponent's forehead. Then, with a shove, Frank sent him sprawling. The two thugs, muttering threats, retreated into an alley. The Hardys headed straight towards their hotel.

"Listen, Joe," Frank said, "we've got to plan some strategy. We're getting nowhere in a hurry."

They were about to mount the steps to the hotel's front door, when a grizzled, gaunt, shifty-eyed man approached them. "Oh—oh, this guy wants a handout," Joe said in a low voice. "He must be king of the down-and-outers."

Despite the warm weather, the man wore a long, threadbare overcoat which nearly touched the ground. His brown hair was streaked with grey and slicked back. A dead cigarette dangled from one corner of his mouth.

"Whatcha say boys, whatcha say!" mumbled the man. "How about a dime for a cup o' coffee?"

"Oh, we might as well," Joe whispered. "It'll be worth it to get rid of him."

"Wait a minute." Frank addressed the beggar.

"Have you been around this neighbourhood long?"

The beggar's long, sharp nose twitched and his foxy-looking eyes nearly closed with mirth as he said with a chuckle, "Long! I'll say—I was born here."

"Then you must know all the people on this block. Right?" Frank queried.

"Sure do. You lookin' for somebody special?"

"Yes, a man named Milo Matlack."

Frank and Joe watched closely for the stranger's reaction. His brows furrowed deeply and his eyes rolled from side to side, as if searching his memory.

"Yeah, I know Matlack," the man finally said.

"Can you tell us where he is?" Joe put in eagerly. "It's important."

The tramp rubbed his fingertips over the mouth-eaten lapels of his coat with evident satisfaction.

"So—you wanna know where Milo Matlack is eh?"

"That's the idea," Frank said somewhat sharply, realizing the man was purposely delaying an answer.

"Well, I can tell you." The tramp thrust his grizzled chin at Frank. "I can tell you—for a price!"

· 5 ·

Dead End

JOE HARDY could barely control his irritation. He opened his mouth to protest, but his brother muttered, "Cool it."

Frank then calmly turned to the man. "What is your price, Mr—"

"Prince. Mortimer Prince is my name, and my price is a hundred dollars."

"No. That's out!" Frank said in disgust, and began to mount the steps.

Mortimer Prince tugged at Frank's arm. "We can bargain, can't we?" he said with a shrug. "So you ain't got a hundred dollars. How about fifty?"

"I wouldn't give you even a dime," Frank said icily, shrugging off the grimy hand.

"All right, all right, don't get mad," the tramp said hastily. "Tell you what—I'll settle for some grub."

"It's a bargain," Frank said quickly. "All you can eat if you tell us where to find Milo Matlack."

Mortimer Prince grinned cheerily and beckoned the boys to follow him. Halfway down the block he ushered them into a dingy place called "Jack's" The three took seats at a small round table.

The vagrant blithely ordered six hamburgers and a large plate of baked beans. As he dived into the food, the boys plied him with questions. But Mortimer did not reply.

"Can't talk while I'm eatin'," he mumbled through a mouthful of meat.

The Hardys waited with growing impatience. With a huge sigh of relish, Mortimer swallowed the last of the beans, wiped his mouth on his coat sleeve, then asked the boys for pencil and paper.

"I'll keep my promise," he said. "I'll show you how to find Matlack."

Frank produced a pencil and Joe a piece of paper, which the tramp took into his grubby hands. "I'll draw you a map where the—er—treasure is," he said.

"You mean Milo Matlack?" Joe said quizzically.

"Yeah, he's the treasure you're lookin' for, ain't he?"

"Go ahead. Write," Frank said.

The Hardys watched as the pencil moved, outlining a diagram of streets. Mortimer Prince sniffed and rubbed his nose. "Look, you fellows follow the arrow to this place marked X, see? That's where Matlack is."

"Okay." Frank folded the map and tucked it in his shirt pocket.

"Now I'd like some dessert," Prince said. "Three scoops of ice cream'll do me."

When he was served, the vagrant ate the ice cream with gusto, but paused occasionally to complain that it was too cold for his teeth. To the Hardys' great relief, he finished soon and stood up, proffering his hand to the boys. "No hard feelin's. We're fair an' square."

Frank paid the bill, and the young detectives and their strange guest parted company.

"Leapin' lizards!" Joe exclaimed, as he and Frank set off down the street. "They say you can meet any and all kinds in New York. And boy, I believe it!"

Frank laughed. Then, suddenly, he wheeled and grasped his brother's arm. "Joe, look!"

Reflected in a store window, next to them, was the monkey-like figure of their rooftop assailant! Both boys swung round. The monkey man, on the other side of the street, stood staring at them!

Impulsively Joe dashed across the road. A horn blared. Brakes screeched. A taxi, bearing down on Joe, stopped a hairbreadth from his flying legs. The driver, red-faced, leaned out of the window and shook his fist at Joe.

"You bird brain! That's a quick way to get to the graveyard!"

Frank hastened to his brother's side, glancing about for the monkey man, but he had disappeared again.

"Joe, next time watch it!" Frank chided him.

"I'll say," the angry taximan agreed. "Guys like you make it hard for a man tryin' to earn an honest livin'."

"Okay, okay, I'm sorry," said Joe. "We'll give you some business, anyhow."

The Hardys hopped into the taxi and Frank showed the driver the map drawn by the tramp. "Can you take us to the place marked X?"

"It's over on Long Island," the man said. "Cost you a fat fare."

The driver sped off uptown, through a tunnel, and finally emerged on to a broad highway. Presently he turned off and half an hour later slowed down at a small cemetery. To the Hardys' astonishment, the driver turned into the cemetery entrance, stopped, and pointed to the X on the map.

"This is it, fellers." With a wink at Joe and a chuckle,

he added, "You got to the graveyard after all, didn't you?"

Joe smiled weakly at the gruesome joke. Then the boys paid the driver and stepped out.

"Have fun!" The driver waved and roared off.

"For Pete's sake!" Joe fumed. "I had a feeling that Mortimer would trick us."

"I wouldn't say he did," Frank replied. "Sure, this is a cemetery, but maybe Matlack works here as a gardener or gravedigger."

They approached a small brown building marked "Office." The door was ajar and the boys stepped inside. Behind a desk sat a portly man with a fringe of white hair like a halo about his head, bushy eyebrows, and a hooked nose which reminded the Hardys of the well-known puppet character, Punch.

"Are you boys looking for a relative?" the man asked solicitously. "I'm the superintendent here."

"Not exactly," Frank replied, barely smothering a smile.

"We're looking for Mr Milo Matlack," Joe spoke up. "Have we come to the right place?"

"Indeed you have. Our groundsman can show you."

He led the boys outside and pointed across the gravel lane. A man in overalls was pruning a row of shrubbery. Before the Hardys could walk over, a funeral cortège drove slowly through the entrance gates.

"Sorry," said the superintendent, "guess you fellows will have to wait." He excused himself and re-entered the office.

The procession was a long one and the Hardys counted fifteen limousines as they slowly drove past. Then the boys hastened across to the groundsman. He readily agreed to take them to Milo Matlack. The trio walked along the gravel lane to the rear of the cemetery. The boys' guide paused at a low, flat area.

Frank and Joe looked about. They could see nobody. "Where's Matlack?" asked Joe.

"Maybe he's having lunch," Frank said.

This remark brought a look of shocked disbelief to the face of the groundsman.

"L-lunch?" he quavered.

Puzzled, the boys followed him in silence to a grave which looked comparatively new. Frank and Joe bent down to examine the headstone. The brothers sucked in their breath sharply and Frank gasped out, "Dead! Milo Matlack—dead!"

·6·

An Insulting Warning

THE Hardys' prime suspect dead! Frank and Joe looked at each other, their mouths agape with bewilderment.

Noting the boys' queer expressions, the workman asked, "Were you friends of the deceased?"

"Oh, no," Joe replied. "Milo Matlack was a—"

"Yes, yes, I know," the man interrupted. "But believe me, Milo repented of his crimes. He became very religious while in prison. Was a handy-man here, very diligent worker, too."

The brothers thanked the groundsman for his trouble and returned to the office. Here Joe asked the manager if Matlack had met his death at the hands of old gangland enemies.

"No," was the reply. The superintendent explained that Milo had become ill soon after the death of his sister and had passed away quietly one night.

"Bad ticker, I believe," the superintendent said, thumping his chest. "I think his heart just plumb gave out."

Outside the cemetery grounds, the Hardys looked at each other sheepishly, their hands thrust deep in their pockets.

"Well—Mortimer Prince must be doubled up laughing at us," Joe said bitterly. "For this joke we bought him lunch!"

Frank tried to sound cheerful. "I realize our deductions have been knocked out of orbit, but at least we know Matlack's off our list."

"I feel like a goof," Joe admitted. "Here we tackle a case for Dad, and we've come across nothing but dead ends."

"If we don't get on the ball pretty soon," Frank remarked, "we'll be low sleuths on the totem pole!"

The Hardys decided to walk for a while before returning to Manhattan. As they strode briskly along, they reviewed every aspect of the mystery. If Matlack was not their man, why was his record stolen from Radley? And why had Fenton Hardy taken Matlack's files with him to Kentucky?

"The answers probably are in Dad's missing briefcase," Frank surmised. "Maybe his dossier on Matlack would help to solve the puzzle."

"You're right. But that briefcase could be anywhere in or out of Kentucky right now."

For the next ten minutes the brothers walked along in silence. Then Frank said, "One thing is certain. Dad's enemies have a super-intelligence system. They didn't waste a minute picking up our trail, and seem to know everything we've planned at home or in New York."

"Which means," Joe said, "that monkey man is one of the gang." He suggested that they return to Bayport. "If we can track down their spy network there," Joe added, "it might put us on the right trail."

Frank hailed a passing taxi, and after a speedy ride, the driver let them out in front of their hotel. Frank paid the fare and turned to his brother.

"Let's case this block first!"

"You're right! That monkey man might still be spying on us."

The boys separated, each sauntering along opposite sides of the street. As inconspicuously as possible, they surveyed the rooftops, and carefully watched for any suspicious motion behind the dirt-streaked windows.

Joe was passing the house where Matlack had lived, when the front door opened. Out stepped the slovenly landlady, still wearing the pink housecoat. She held a broom in her hands and began to sweep the steps. Joe bounded up to her and Frank followed.

"Milo Matlack's dead. Why didn't you tell us?" Joe asked.

Instead of replying, the woman scurried into the house and locked the door.

"Boy, she's really scared," Frank declared. "Somebody has threatened her to keep her quiet."

"But why—if Matlack is out of the picture?"

"To keep us on the wrong track!"

Frank and Joe walked across the street and posted themselves in the doorway of a vacant store in case any suspicious person showed up at No. 47. Nothing happened, however, and the landlady did not reappear. The boys also kept an eye out for the vagrant who had tricked them, but the grubby drifter was not to be seen among the passers-by.

Finally they returned to the hotel. The desk clerk handed Frank the room key. "You two checking out? Otherwise you'll owe us for another day."

"We're leaving in fifteen minutes."

In their musty room the Hardys threw the few possessions they had brought into their overnight bags. Joe said to himself, "Shaving kit, tooth-paste—" His mental check stopped suddenly when he picked up his red-handled tooth-brush from the side of the wash-basin. A white paper was wrapped around it, held securely by an elastic band.

"Frank, look at this!" Joe slipped off the elastic and opened the paper. Printed on it in crude letters was *"Warning—Bayport is for Brats."* It was signed with an odd-looking M with three spiral loops.

Frank gritted his teeth. "If Matlack weren't dead, I'd swear he left this warning."

"It's a dirty insult! Bayport for Brats, eh?" Joe exploded. "We'll show them."

The brothers quickly finished packing, hastened downstairs with their bags, and questioned the desk clerk. He denied knowledge of the toothbrush warning. A silly grin came over his face. "Say, maybe some joker did it before you left home."

The Hardys made no comment. Handing over the key, they left.

"That was a bright theory!" Joe said sarcastically, as the two walked away from the hotel.

Frank stopped at the first public telephone booth and contacted Jack Wayne. The pilot told them the plane was in readiness and that he would take off immediately to meet them at Kennedy. Exactly on schedule Jack set down the Hardy plane at the airfield and the boys climbed into the cabin.

The flight to Bayport was smooth and fast. From the airport, the young sleuths drove directly to the hospital. It was past visiting hours, but they were allowed to look in briefly on Mr Hardy. Much to Frank and Joe's relief, they found their father slightly improved, but as yet unable to talk clearly.

Back home, Joe called Sam Radley and told of their experiences in New York. He was surprised to learn that Matlack was dead.

"This mystery is a real puzzler," Sam remarked. "At least you two found out somebody's worried by your sleuthing."

Sam said no further clues had turned up locally as to the prowler's identity. Then the Hardys checked with their pals. None of the four had detected anyone suspicious near the hospital or the Hardy house.

The following morning Frank and Joe discussed what their next move should be. From the living-room came assorted thumps and clicking noises. Aunt Gertrude was assembling the vacuum cleaner with her usual vigour.

"Goodness gracious, Gertrude!" came Mrs Hardy's voice. "We cleaned thoroughly just a few days ago!"

The boys grinned and went into the living-room. Joe squinted his eyes, as if inspecting the room. "Aunty, relax, there's not a cobweb in sight!"

Aunt Gertrude pursed her lips. "Don't be funny," she said tartly. "There happens to be a spot on the ceiling in one corner of your father's study." With an accusing look at her nephews, she added, "You and your friends were the last to use it."

"Wow!" Joe said. "Aunty, I'll bet you could spot a speck of dust ten miles away. Better be careful, though, it might be a beetle!"

"Humph!" Aunt Gertrude gathered her equipment and carried it up the carpeted stairs.

Suddenly an electrifying thought flashed through Frank's brain. He ran upstairs. Aunt Gertrude was about to enter the detective's study when Frank grabbed her. The startled woman gasped.

"What—?" was all she could get out, because Frank clapped a hand over her mouth and dragged his flabbergasted aunt into the hall.

·7·

Bug Bait

GERTRUDE HARDY's eyes bulged with fright as Frank kept a hand clapped over her mouth and half carried her down the stairway into the living room.

"Good grief!" exclaimed Joe. "What—"

"Sh, sh!" Frank whispered frantically. "Don't make a sound." He released his aunt and led the trembling woman into the kitchen. The others followed.

Mrs Hardy spoke first. "What on earth are you up to, Frank?"

"I know," Aunt Gertrude said tartly as she smoothed her dishevelled hair and set her spectacles straight. "Frank has gone stark raving mad, that's what!" She glared at her elder nephew.

"I'm sorry Aunty," Frank said soothingly. "You see—I think that dirt spot on the ceiling you're talking about is a bug."

"Oh! It really is a beetle! Ugh!"

"Not that kind of bug," Frank went on with a smile. " 'Bug' is slang for a hidden microphone."

"So that's how the crooks knew all about our plans!" Joe whispered hoarsely.

"But that seems impossible!" Mrs Hardy said. "No outsider has been here recently!"

"Except Mr Kenfield," Aunt Gertrude said. She

had calmed down, but there was a look of deep concern on her face.

"Hmm. You said you heard his ladder against the house," Frank reflected. "Joe, let's go take a look at that spot."

After cautioning the two women to keep their voices low, Frank and Joe kicked off their shoes and padded up the stairs. They went into the study and looked at the speck. No larger in circumference than a pencil, it protruded an eighth of an inch from the ceiling, so close to the corner that it might not ordinarily have been seen.

Frank put his finger to his lips and beckoned Joe out into the hall. There he whispered into his brother's ear. "It's a listening device all right. The transmitter must have been installed in our attic."

Silently Frank opened the door to the attic stairway, and the boys tiptoed up. One window was opened halfway, and near it the Hardys spotted a small radio transmitter inserted between two floorboards. Impulsively, Joe reached down to yank it out, but Frank restrained him.

Retracing their steps, the boys hastened back to the kitchen.

"Well, what kind of beetle is it?" Aunt Gertrude asked.

"The big-eared type," Joe replied. He quickly reached for the phone wall extension and called Mr Kenfield. He asked for the roofer to come over immediately.

In about ten minutes the roofer parked his truck in front of the house. Mr Kenfield, short and portly, was wearing his work clothes.

"Hello, Frank, Joe," he said, as the boys stepped outside to meet him. "I suppose it's the garage roof you want me to look over, right?"

"No," Joe said. "We'd like to ask you some questions."

"Shoot."

The boys' first query was whether or not the roofer had gone into the attic. He said no; that he had examined the roof from the outside only. "But the electrical inspector," Mr Kenfield continued, "went into your attic."

"Who?" asked Frank.

"An electrical inspector. He said you had some rewiring done, and he'd been called to look it over."

The brothers exchanged glances. This was news to them!

"How did he get in?" Joe queried.

"Asked if he could use my ladder. It was okay with me. You know I'm willing to oblige."

"Can you describe this fellow for us?" Frank asked.

"Why, sure. He was short, thin, kind of bandy-legged and agile. You should've seen him zip up that ladder! Like a—"

"Like a monkey?" Joe put in.

"Yes, sure, that's it! I was going to say monkey myself, but I didn't want to insult him if he's a friend of yours."

Joe could not help smiling. "He's not."

Frank concluded that the roofer was not to blame. He had had no reason to suspect the "inspector" was a fraud.

"Thanks a lot, Mr Kenfield," Frank said. "That's all we wanted to know."

"Glad to help, any time."

As soon as the roofer had left, Frank exclaimed, "Joe, now we have a chance to turn the tables! We'll 'confer' in Dad's study and feed the bug false information."

"Great!" Joe said with enthusiasm.

"That way we can tell if the mike's still in operation, and even lead the crooks on a wild goose chase," Frank added.

First the boys told their mother and Aunt Gertrude what they had learned. "So, if you see the monkey man anywhere around, call us right away," Frank said. "And if we're not here, notify Chief Collig."

Aunt Gertrude shuddered. "First bugs, now a monkey! Oh dear!"

Frank and Joe put their plan into operation. They walked up the stairs noisily and entered their father's study, chatting loudly.

"Well, we've got the dope on them," Frank said. "Let's fly down to Kentucky."

"Right away?" Joe asked. He looked up towards the microphone and winked at his brother.

"You bet. We can get ready in a jiffy." Frank made the telephone clatter as he lifted it from its cradle. Then, pressing the button down, he dialled and pretended to talk to their pilot.

"Jack Wayne? . . . This is Frank Hardy. Get her fuelled up. We're taking off for Kentucky this afternoon."

Frank hung up with a noise that was sure to be picked up by the bug, then added, "Come on, Joe. We'll give those crooks a hard time."

The boys confided in Mrs Hardy what the · had done and Frank told her, "We're going out to Chet's. If

Jack should phone, please have him buzz us there."

"All right. I hope your ruse works."

The Mortons lived on a farm. The rambling homestead, surrounded by rolling countryside, was a favourite haunt of the Hardy boys. The foremost attraction was Iola Morton, Chet's dark-haired sister, whom Joe regarded as his best girl. Her friend Callie Shaw, a slender, blonde, lithe girl, was often on the farm, which suited Frank very well since Callie was his favourite date.

Today, as they pulled up at the house, Frank beamed. "There's Callie's car."

Joe's face lit up. "That means Iola's at home. We're both in luck."

The Hardys hopped out and looked for their friends. Suddenly they heard a dull clunk from behind the barn, followed by several giggles. "Oh, Chet, that was marvellous!" came Callie's voice.

"Wonder what Chet's up to now," Joe said.

He and Frank trotted round a henhouse and reached the rear of the barn in time to see Chet, in a bulky sweater, bend down to pick up a heavy metal ball. The two girls sat in the grass, their backs propped against the barn wall. Seeing Frank and Joe, they immediately jumped up.

"Hi!" dark-eyed Iola called gaily. "You're just in time to see the exhibition of the year, by no less a person than my brother!"

"Aw, cut it out," said Chet.

"No, really," Callie insisted in mock seriousness. "Chet, you are destined o be a fabulous shot-putter."

The Hardys stood grinning. From time to time their stout friend would plunge enthusiastically into a new sport or hobby. As a rule, the new interest was short-lived.

Frank and Joe flopped down beside the girls. "C'mon, muscles." Joe urged. "Let's see you hurl."

With deliberation, Chet walked back to a circle he had marked out on the grass. He picked up a book lying there and studied it intently. The title was *Proper Methods for Putting the Shot.*

"I'm glad to see you concentrating so hard, Chet old boy," Joe needled.

"Kid all you want," retorted Chet, mopping a trickle of sweat from his brow. "Don't forget, the Olympics are coming up and Uncle Sam needs shot-putters!"

Iola finally spoke up in defence of her brother. "No fooling, boys, Chet's really getting good at this."

The stout boy threw out his expansive chest, balanced the shot in his right hand, and began to move his shoulders rhythmically.

"Let her fly!" Frank called.

Chet spun around and released the sphere.

"Wow!" Joe cried out. The ball arced directly over the henhouse.

Crash! With the sound of splintering wood, mingled with the squawking of the fowls, the metal ball pierced the roof, leaving a jagged hole.

The noise brought Mrs Morton to the back steps of the farmhouse. "Chester!" she called out. "What's all that racket?"

"Oh nothing to worry about, Mum," Chet replied hastily. "Say, Mum, would you like to have chicken for supper?" But Mrs Morton had already gone inside. Fortunately, as the young people discovered, Chet's mighty missile had missed the chickens.

"Chet, you've got a great throw," said Joe. "I mean it. What power!"

"Yeah, but what a long time it'll take me to fix the henhouse roof!" Chet groaned.

The young people's laughter was interrupted by Mrs Morton's calling:

"Frank! Telephone!"

He rushed into the house, his face flushed with excitement. Joe ran after him.

"Hello. . . . Jack? . . . I thought it might be you."

Joe stood by tensely. Then Frank burst out, "Just as I figured!"

· 8 ·

New Strategy

JACK WAYNE had reported to Frank that someone using a high-powered rifle had fired a bullet into the propeller of the Hardy plane. It would take several days to get a new one.

"The gunman must have shot from a good distance," Jack said. "He probably hid in the foliage outside the field."

"Our enemy really wants to stop us," said Frank.

"But how did you know something like this might happen?" the pilot asked.

The young sleuth told him about their ruse and the events leading up to it. "Jack," he added, "this shows we can turn that bug to our own advantage."

"Right," Wayne replied, "and perhaps lead the crooks into a trap. But the next time tell me, eh?"

After Frank had apologised for the oversight, he relayed the entire conversation to Joe, Chet, and the girls.

"Ha!" Joe was gleeful. "They sure went for our bait."

"Now it's time to plan new tactics," Frank said. "We'll get the other fellows together for a meeting today."

"And leave us out?" Callie gave a small pout.

"We were going to invite you boys to a dance," Iola said, dimpling.

Joe brightened. "A dance? When?"

"Next Wednesday. It's the annual Fresh Air Camp Benefit Ball," said Callie. "We were going to buy the tickets and surprise you."

"That'd be great, but we can't make it then," Frank said regretfully. "We'll probably be far away from here."

"Like Kentucky, maybe," Joe put in. "Can we take a rain check?"

The girls were disappointed, but they wished the young detectives well and offered to help in any way they could.

"Okay," replied Frank. "Can you suggest a good place for us to hold a secret meeting?"

"How about Tony Prito's?" asked Callie. "They have a terrific basement room. Remember the party we had there last spring?"

"Perfect," Joe replied. He immediately telephoned the Prito residence. Tony was not at home, but his mother answered.

When Joe made his request, Mrs Prito said, "By all means, you boys come over. And save your appetites—I'll make spaghetti and meatballs for all of you. You can hold your meeting after dinner. We'll eat at seven o'clock."

"Thanks, Mrs Prito, but—"

"No trouble at all. I'll tell Tony as soon as he gets home."

"That's real nice of you, Mrs Prito," said Joe. "Thank you."

When Chet heard of the dinner plans, he was delighted. "Great!" he declared. "Spaghetti and meatballs! Just what I need for building shot-putting muscles!"

Telephone calls were quickly made to Biff and Phil, who said they would come. Shortly before seven that evening, Frank and Joe drove to the Prito home, located on the north side of town. Chet Morton, who was the last to arrive, explained that he had practised shot-putting until an hour before, just so that he would be certain to have an appetite!

This statement tickled Phil Cohen. "Chet, you could work up an appetite just twirling your thumbs!"

Tony explained that his father had gone to Kentucky the previous day. Mrs Prito looked troubled. "More bad luck on the road project," she said, shaking her head. "I don't know when it will end. Of course, the worst of it is your father's llness, Frank and Joe!"

For a while, however, the mood of worry was dispelled by the sumptuous spread that Mrs Prito had prepared. The meal started with antipasto, followed by thick minestrone soup. By the time the boys had eaten their first helping of spaghetti and meatballs, most of their hunger had been satisfied. As usual, Chet was the exception.

Mrs Prito watched with a broad smile as Chet accepted a second generous portion.

"Building up my strength," he said, spearing a succulent meatball. After desert of fresh fruit, the boys thanked their hostess.

"Wow, that was some feast!" said Chet, patting his stomach. "I'll be a champion shot-putter yet!"

Biff grinned. "How about a little exercise before we start the meeting?" Everyone agreed, and the boys clattered down to the basement.

In the spacious recreation room the Hardys, Phil, and Tony decided on a billiard game, while Biff and

Chet trotted off to the ping-pong table at the far end.

"This'll get rid of that stuffed feeling, Biff," assured the stout boy.

After a few minutes of warming up, the two engaged in a furious tilt. The sound of the bouncing balls mingled with the jolly banter of the billiard players.

As Frank lined up a shot to send the nine ball into the side pocket, a terrific crash filled the basement. This was followed by a loud "oof."

Startled, the other boys' companions wheeled round to face the ping-pong table. It lay flat on the floor, with hapless Chet sprawled out across it. Red-faced, as the others roared with laughter, he picked himself up.

"What happened?" Tony asked.

"I fooled him with a spin shot," Biff said. "Good old Chet leaned over too far and that did it."

Frank found that except for one splintered leg, no damage had been done to the table.

Joe and Tony quickly got tools from a work-bench and repaired the table leg.

"Okay, fellows," Frank said finally. "Before Chet has any more accidents, let's get down to business."

First, Tony took the precaution of posting his German shepherd dog outside the basement door.

"Axel will warn us if anybody comes snooping around," he said.

The boys seated themselves in a partitioned-off den-study, and Frank opened the discussion.

"Joe and I will lay our cards on the table. We've met with nothing but setbacks ever since we took over Dad's case."

"You're not giving up?" Tony Prito put in quickly.

"Of course not!" Joe assured him. "There's no mystery that can't be solved, if it's worked on long and hard enough."

"Right, "Chet Morgan said sagely. "You two should know."

Phil Cohen winked at Biff. "A hunch tells me you Hardys got us together to decide on a plan of action."

Frank smiled. "You're right, Phil. You fellows have always stuck with us when the going got rough."

Chet Morton nodded vigorously. "What else are pals for?"

"I'm glad to hear that," Joe said, "because now we come to the heart of the matter."

The Hardys were silent for a moment as Frank looked from face to face. "Joe and I," he said, in measured words, "are asking each of you to join us on a dangerous mission."

Chet's eyebrows arched like the trajectory of a soaring shot. "Dangerous? Where?"

"Kentucky."

The Hardys' friends exchanged excited glances.

"Yes," Joe said, "let's go to Kentucky and find out more about that sabotaged bridge and who dry-gulched Dad."

The Hardys thoroughly briefed the others on their sleuthing so far, including the New York trip. They had just concluded when Tony's dog began barking.

"Something's going on!" said Tony. He dashed to the basement door, opened it, and peered into the darkness.

The big German shepherd was leaping up at the shadowy figure of a man near the basement window!

·9·

Fake Names

"DOWN, Axel!" A deep voice came out of the darkness, followed by a happy whimper from the German Shepherd.

"It's my father!" Tony exclaimed.

A sturdy-looking man, the dog bounding at his heels, stepped into the basement.

"Hello, Mr Prito." Joe grinned. "For a minute we thought you were a prowler."

The broad-shouldered contractor's face, ruddy from years of outdoor work, creased in a smile,

"Not guilty. When I saw all those cars parked in the driveway, I thought maybe a political rally was in progress here."

"Frank Hardy for Mayor," Phil quipped.

Everyone laughed, then sobered as Frank spoke up. "We were having a powwow about your road job, Mr Prito."

The group adjourned to the den, where the contractor pulled up a chair and sat down wearily.

"I'm afraid we are licked."

"Did something else go wrong, Dad?" Tony asked.

"My men started to repair the bridge, and it collapsed again. This time we found an acetylene torch was used to cut through the stress points of the girders.

The cuts were covered with putty filler and painted over to resemble rivets—so of course no one noticed anything wrong until the structure gave way."

"Was anyone hurt?" Chet put in.

"Fortunately, no—they scrambled to safety in time." Mr Prito sighed. "Unless we can find out who is causing the sabotage, and prove it, I may have to give up the whole project."

"And lose all that money?" Biff said.

Joe spoke up. "Frank and I were just asking the fellows if they could go to Kentucky with us. Our idea is to get jobs on the road crew and maybe then solve this mystery

"A bold idea. What is the rest of your plan?"

Frank first of all inquired if Mr Prito had a trusted foreman who could handle the hiring of the boys.

"Yes, John Losi. I sent him down to Kentucky temporarily, because the regular hiring agent, a local man named Bond Deemer, is on a week's leave from the job."

"What could be better!" said Joe.

Then the Hardys went on to explain their scheme. Each of the boys would get a different job. Tony could be a mechanic for road-building equipment, such as graders and earth-moving machines.

"Big Biff here could man a truck," said Joe, and Frank suggested that Phil sign on as a timekeeper, to see whether anyone stayed away from work for any length of time.

Phil grinned happily. "Great! That'll give me time to sketch."

"Hey, what about me?" demanded Chet.

"A labourer," Frank said. "That'll really build up

your muscles—while your picking up gossip from the other workers."

"Sort of like a spy, eh?"

"That's right," Tony interjected. "Secret agent oo8, with the accent on the a-t-e."

Chet grinned and accepted his new role. "And what may I ask, are Frank and Joe Hardy going to be? Spy supervisors?"

"Espionage foremen, so to speak," quipped Tony.

"Not quite pal." Frank explained that the Hardys would work with the bridge crew. In that way, they could keep close tabs on the workmen in case one or two might be connected with sabotaging the project.

"But everybody knows the name Hardy," Mr Prito said. "The saboteurs would soon catch on that you are Fenton's sons."

In answer Frank pulled out a piece of paper from his pocket. "We've already worked that out, by each of us keeping his first name and changing only the surname."

Joe added, "The payroll records can be corrected for the government later, can't they, Mr Prito?"

"Yes, indeed."

Frank unfolded the paper and spread it on the table.

"You picked our fake names already?" Biff asked with a grin.

"Sure thing. Listen:

Frank Teller
Joe Jensen
Chet Ball
Biff McGuire
Tony Gonzales
Phil Rubinow."

"A masterpiece!" Phil declared. "Joe, you're blond like a Scandinavian, and Tony could pass for Spanish."

"But what about Chet Ball?" asked Biff.

"Oh, I get it," said Chet. "That metal ball I've been shot-putting."

The boys began trying out their aliases on one another.

"Biff McGuire," said Biff. "Not bad, sounds like a real rugged character."

"And we'll need a few on this trip," declared Joe.

By now the Hardys had generated such enthusiasm among their friends that Mr Prito finally acceded to the plan.

"I'ts a risky one remember!" the contractor warned. "But good luck. You can reach me here if necessary. I have several other projects going."

Frank and Joe suggested that the other boys leave Bayport one by one, at varying times, in order to avoid attracting attention.

"We're leaving on the early bus tomorrow morning," said Frank. "We'll see you all in Kentucky."

On the way home Joe was jubilant. Now that they had hoodwinked their enemies by their own microphone, he was sure the criminals could be thrown completely off the trail.

Joe laughed. "Maybe we can say we're going fishing in Canada, or something like that."

"I hope we can fool them, but let's not count our chickens too soon," Frank said, as they drove into the garage.

So exuberant were the two boys that they dashed through the kitchen and raced upstairs to their father's study. Frank closed the door, winked at his brother, and mustered up his most doleful voice.

"Joe," he said, "this case is too much for us. I think we should quit and let the police handle everything."

With a mocking expression, Joe jabbed his finger over the back of his shoulder towards the bug on the ceiling. "Right, Frank. We know when we're licked."

Just then there was a quiet knock at the door. When Joe opened it, Mrs Hardy beckoned them into the hall and down the stairs. In the living-room she whispered, "You two came in so fast, I couldn't tell you."

"Tell us what?" queried Frank, noting his mother's look of alarm.

"Come, I'll show you.

Aunt Gertrude joined them. She too, seemed fearful.

"Oh, do be careful, Frank and Joe," Miss Hardy said in a strained voice.

Joe scratched his head. "What's this all about?"

Mrs Hardy walked into the kitchen, picked up a flashlight from the table, and led her sons into the side yard. She played the beam up the house. Her sons gasped. A light nylon rope, looped around the chimney top, ran past an attic window to within a foot of the ground.

"Gertrude and I noticed it when we came home from the hospital," Mrs Hardy explained.

"Great gophers!" Joe exclaimed. "Somebody climbed up there!" In a moment the boys were bounding through the kitchen, into the hall, up the stairs and into the attic. Frank turned on the switch and the attic was flooded with light. The Hardys took one look and and groaned. The radio transmitter was gone!

The trickers had been tricked!

Joe hastened to the window near the chimney and looked out. The nylon rope dangled only inches away from the sill.

"The monkey man!" Frank exclaimed.

The boys looked at each other, sick with fury over the way they had been outmanoeuvred. Suddenly there was a crash, followed by a tinkling of glass.

"It's downstairs," Frank said. "Come on!"

The boys ran to the first floor. They arrived in the living-room to find Aunt Gertrude and Mrs Hardy standing motionless, their faces registering shock.

"What happened? What—"

Joe pointed to the living-room window, which had a large, jagged hole in the centre. The boys' gaze travelled to the rug, on which lay a large ball-bearing with a paper wrapped loosely around it.

Aunt Gertrude found her voice. "Thieves! Criminals! Murderers!" she cried shrilly.

Frank snatched up the paper, and with hearts pounding, he and Joe read the message: "*Wise guys stay in Bayport.*" It was signed with the three-looped letter M.

· 10 ·

Monkey on a String

THE latest threat from the Hardys' enemies only served to stiffen the boys' resolve. Frank and Joe quietly left the house and stealthily searched the grounds. But they discovered no clue to the missile hurler.

Frank stopped at the dangling nylon rope and yanked it hard. It was firmly fastened around the chimney.

"The fellow must be great with a lariat," said Joe. "Wonder why he left it here."

Frank had a theory. If the intruder had been surprised by Mrs Hardy and Aunt Gertrude, he might have shinned down a drainpipe on the other side of the house.

"Without time to unfasten and take his rope," Joe added.

"Right."

The boys had a whispered conference.

"Okay!" Joe said. "Let's try it!"

They confided their plans for the Kentucky trip to their mother and Aunt Gertrude. The women, although apprehensive, did not oppose the idea.

"We found your father better this evening," said Mrs Hardy. "But he's still not fully conscious. I suppose he would want you to take his place."

Next, Joe phoned Radley, telling him of their plans. Sam approved heartily and wished the boys success.

"I'll keep an eye on your dad and your house," he promised. "Keep me posted."

The boys then got out their suitcases, and as they packed, cut off all the telltale labels from their clothing.

"Have you got the binoculars?" asked Frank.

"Roger. And our miniature radio transmitter." They were about to shut their bags when Mrs Hardy and Aunt Gertrude came into the room.

"Do you have your heavy sweaters?" Miss Hardy asked with an air of authority. "Kentucky isn't Miami, you know."

"But, Aunty, we're not going to the North Pole!" Joe protested. "Besides, it's summer."

"Never mind. It still gets chilly in the woods at night," she insisted.

"All right," Frank agreed. He reached in the closet and pulled out two heavy woollen sweaters which he and Joe hurriedly packed.

"And now, Mother," Frank said, "will you drive us to the bus depot? We can catch the midnight bus."

After receiving parting admonitions and a hug from their aunt, the boys and Mrs Hardy got into the car and soon were at the terminal.

"This bus to Kentucky goes via Pittsburgh, Mum," Frank said. "Goodbye and don't worry."

He and Joe embraced their mother, then swung aboard. A few minutes later, with a roar of its diesel motor, the vehicle swung out on to the main street. But it had gone only four blocks when Frank tapped the driver on the shoulder.

"We'd like to get off here, please."

"What? We've hardly started," argued the driver. "This isn't a local, y'know."

"It's very important," Joe said solemnly.

"Okay, okay."

The bus stopped at the next corner and the boys hopped off. They strode rapidly back home, approaching the house cautiously from the rear. Nimbly they hopped a fence into their backyard. Silent as shadows, the Hardys cached their suitcases behind the garage, then crept to a sheltering clump of rhododendrons. Tensely they waited, their eyes fixed on the chimney.

Joe whispered, "Do you really think someone will come back for the rope?"

"Sure."

Earlier Frank had reasoned that their enemy was watching for his opportunity to return to the Hardy home undetected and retrieve the rope. Therefore, he would be more likely to do so if he thought the brothers had left town.

Half an hour passed. Forty-five minutes. Joe glanced into the starry sky and saw that Orion had moved some distance west in the velvety black sky. The boys' muscles ached.

"Frank, I don't think anybody will—"

Joe's words were cut off by a nudge from his brother. The crouching boys peered through the shrubs at a small figure creeping round the side of their house. Joe put his mouth to Frank's ear. "The monkey man!"

"Sh!"

The prowler stopped, listened, then advanced towards the nylon rope. The Hardys were tense with excitement, but dared not move a muscle lest they scare off their enemy. They must capture him at any cost, if their trip to Kentucky were to bring results.

Otherwise, the monkey man would be certain to give away the Hardys' identity, and alert those mixed up in the bridge sabotage.

The intruder waited as if to make sure everyone was safely asleep in the darkened house. Then the man sprang to his full height, which was a scant five feet. Like a cat, he glided up to the rope, seized it, and began virtually walking up the side of the Hardy house.

The boys put their plan into action. Cautiously Joe moved from his hiding place, quietly unlocked the back door, and sped upstairs in the darkness. Frank, meanwhile, darted to the dangling rope and began to pull himself up hand over hand.

The jerk on the rope signalled Frank's presence. The monkey man, now halfway to the roof, uttered a high-pitched cry. The lights in the house blazed on, and Joe stepped out of the attic window close to the rope. He, too, seized the nylon rope and began to slide down it.

The monkey man was caught between the Hardys!

He shrieked in rage and defiance. "You won't get me!"

With that, he crashed through the screen of an open first-floor window. Instantly Frank dropped to the ground. A moment later he heard a scream, a bang, and a thump coming from downstairs. He dashed inside to find the monkey man picking himself up from the hall floor at the bottom of the stairs. Aunt Gertrude stood nearby, brandishing an umbrella.

"Crashed right into me!" she gasped.

Frank made a dive for the intruder. Then Joe, halfway between the ground and first floors, leaped from the stairway and landed on the monkey man's back.

As the trio rolled over and over, the trapped prowler, though small, fought with the fury of a wild animal. His arms and legs writhed like snakes as he tried to escape the Hardys' steel grip.

Dishevelled and bruised, the boys finally subdued the monkey man, and sat astride him. Mrs Hardy had called the police and soon a squad car roared up. A lieutenant entered and snapped handcuffs on the prisoner.

Chief Collig arrived minutes later, having received word of the fracas at his home.

"Do you know this man, Chief?" asked Frank, as the monkey man glowered at his captors.

"I'll say. He's on the wanted list. His name is Monk Smith, an ex-con."

Frank and Joe told Collig of Smith's assault on them in New York. "We figure," Joe added in a low voice, "he fits in somewhere with the bridge mystery Dad was working on."

The chief turned to the prisoner. "Who put you up to this caper, Monk?"

Smith only scowled, and would not reply to this question or to any others.

"Okay, take him down to the lockup," Collig instructed finally. "Maybe he'll sing there."

The police chief said that the ex-convict would be held without bail for a few days, in order to give the Hardys a better chance to work incognito in Kentucky.

After the police car had sped off, the boys took down the rope. "This might come in handy," Joe said as he coiled the light nylon and put it in his suitcase.

In a short time the brothers said goodbye again to their mother and Aunt Gertrude.

The monkey man was caught between the Hardys!

Joe grinned. "This time we're really Kentucky-bound."

He and Frank took a taxi to the bus terminal, and the next bus out. Settling back in the comfortable seats, the weary young sleuths soon fell fast asleep as the bus hummed along the dark highway.

The next day found the Hardys' pals leaving Bayport as arranged, separately and at different times: first, Tony; next, Chet; third, Biff; and Phi was last to depart. Their arrival times were spaced so that over the weekend, each made his way independently to the construction shack of John Losi.

Mr Prito's trusted assistant was expecting them, and without delay assigned the four to their respective jobs. Monday, their first day at work, was a busy one. It was not until Tuesday morning that the Bayporters became worried about the delayed arrival of the Hardy boys. Chet rested on his shovel next to a pile of dirt alongside a section of freshly poured concrete.

"Where are Frank and Joe?" he wondered. "They left before any of us did."

Among the swarms of workers in the densely wooded area, Chet could make out his three cohorts. Tony, stripped to the waist in the hot sun, was repairing a tractor by the roadside. Biff was driving a concrete mixer, while Phil Cohen, busy writing on a clipboard, stood near an abutment of the bridge under construction.

A brusque voice at his elbow startled Chet.

"We'll never build this road with you leaning on your shovel, buster."

The newcomer, a sandy-haired, hard-eyed man, told Chet he was Bond Deemer, the regular hiring agent.

"I just got back this morning before Losi left. When did you come on the job?"

Somewhat taken off guard, Chet stammered, "Well, ah, we—I—got here late on Saturday, when Mr Losi hired me."

"What's your name?"

Chet gulped. "Chet Ball."

"Okay," said Deemer. "I expect a full day's work. Understand?"

Deemer strode off and Chet resumed shovelling. The hefty boy glanced up now and then at his strange surroundings. Across from the road site, set among the pine trees, were five trailers. Four were used as bunk-houses and the fifth, much larger, contained the kitchen and commissary.

Despite his gloomy mood, Chet felt hunger pangs. "Wish it was chow time," he thought. The nearest town, Boonton, was too far away for a quick hop to obtain a sack of hamburgers.

Chet's eyes roved to the wide, gushing stream and the bridge, built halfway across. This was the one, he knew, that twice had collapsed, and now the crew was busy pushing its construction for the third time.

Almost unconsciously, Chet again paused in his work. How could they do any sleuthing without Frank and Joe? he asked himself disconsolately.

"Hey, Ball!" A lantern-jawed man hopped off the cement mixer and strolled towards Chet.

"Wh-who, me?"

"Your name is Ball, isn't it?"

"Yes, Mr Angan," Chet replied hastily.

It hadn't taken the newcomers long to learn that

Robert Angan was the foreman, and a rough taskmaster at that!

"Look, Ball, you're not paid to stand there like the Statue of Liberty! Get to work!"

Embarrassed, Chet dug his shovel deep into the loose dirt. "That's right," Angan needled. "Act like you're alive!"

A few minutes later Chet straightened up to ease his aching back. Across from him he spied two sturdy youths in dungarees hauling a large log on their shoulders. Chet bravely restrained a whoop of joy. *Frank and Joe Hardy!*

Frank, in the lead, gave a slight nod of recognition as he and Joe proceeded towards the bridge. Chet started to whistle, and dirt flew furiously from his shovel.

"Hey, Ball, that's more like it!" yelled Angan.

A shrill blast from a steam whistle signalled the noon hour. Trucks and construction vehicles ground to a halt, and all the workmen headed towards the commissary. Meals were eaten at long, rough-hewn tables inside the trailer. Many of the old-timers sat together, talking and joking as they ate.

Frank, Joe, and their friends managed to find seats near one another, but chatted casually as if they had just met. Across from the Hardys sat a tall hillbilly youth. He had large hands and a long neck, and his Adam's apple bobbed up and down when he swallowed.

"My name is Jensen—Joe Jensen," Joe Hardy said, extending a hand.

The youth looked up shyly from under a shock of brown hair. "Mine's Willy Teeple."

"Live around here?" asked Joe.

"Yup."

The Hardys could see that Willy was not one for conversation. The sentences he spoke were barely longer than one or two words. The foreman, Angan, who happened to be at the boys' table, seemed to take great delight in riding the workmen.

"See here, Gonzales," he said to Tony. "If you don't get that tractor fixed pretty soon, you'll be heading back south of the border!"

"Yes, sir!" Tony replied.

"Don't sir me!" Angan shot back. "Just do what you're hired for."

"Yes, *Mr* Angan."

"As for you, Jensen, you dumb Swede"—Angan turned to Joe—"I noticed you bothering the guys with questions. What are you? A reporter?"

With difficulty Joe held back a retort and mumbled, "Sorry."

Chet, ravenous, reached for a third piece of bread. He changed his mind abruptly as Angan stared at him.

"We don't like heavyweights on our crew!" the foreman said pointedly.

Having finished, Chet rose to leave. As he neared the end of the bench where Angan sat, Chet accidentally jostled the man's elbow, and the cup of coffee he held spilled over the table.

"Dummy!" roared Angan, jumping up. With one hand he grasped the front of Chet's work shirt and twisted it until the buttons nearly popped. His other fist cocked back. "For two cents I'd—"

Without warning, Willy Teeple's big hands grasped the foreman's wrist in a vice-like grip.

"I wouldn't do that, Mr Angan," Willy said softly.

Jailbird Language

WILLY TEEPLE'S grasp prevented Angan's fist from sailing to its mark on Chet's jaw. The foreman released him and swung on Willy. At the same instant, Bond Deemer ran over and forced himself between the two.

"What's the idea of interfering, Teeple?" Deemer thundered. "Angan handles the men around here."

The hillbilly backed off, his face showing no resentment. "Okay, Mr Deemer," he said.

Chet, meanwhile, had stood by half stunned by the foreman's sudden violence. His pals had found it hard not to go to his aid. To their surprise, Angan turned to Chet apologetically.

"I'm sorry Ball," he said. "I shouldn't have lost my temper. But we're in an awful mess around here and my nerves are on edge."

"That's all right, Mr Angan," replied Chet, relieved.

"You know what will happen if our bad luck continues," Angan said, looking about in appeal to the onlooking workmen. "The Prito company will be penalized five hundred dollars a day for every day extra it takes to finish this job beyond the time we've contracted for."

Tony spoke up. "I guess that would just about put Mr Prito out of business, wouldn't it?"

"I'm afraid so," Angan replied, "and Prito's a good guy."

"Okay, break it up," Deemer ordered impatiently. "Back to work."

With a scuffle of heavy boots, the workmen filed out of the commissary. On the way Chet thanked Willy for coming to his rescue. The gangling youth gave a quick nod and turned off. Soon power shovels were chugging and earth-moving equipment went bouncing over the rough, unfinished portions of the highway. Working together, Frank and Joe found an opportunity to discuss the work gang.

"It's hard to tell who's friend or foe," Joe remarked. "But I guess it's too soon to form any suspicions."

The Hardys agreed that Angan, although hot-tempered, seemed to be all right.

"He was actually sorry for Mr Prito," Frank observed.

Deemer's not especially good-natured, either," said Joe. "But he seems okay."

The Hardys' contact with their pals for the rest of the day was brief and surreptitious.

"Anything new?" Frank asked, as he passed close to Chet.

"No."

The same question, whispered in passing, to Phil, Biff, and Tony also produced a negative reply.

After the evening meal, Frank drew his brother aside. "We've got to do some sleuthing tonight," he said.

The Hardys sauntered among the workmen lounging about, some smoking, others chatting in front of the bunk trailers. Frank sat on a tree stump while Joe flopped on a grassy knoll nearby. Soon they were casually approached by Tony.

"Hi, there," he said in a loud voice. "How do you like working here?" Then in lowered tones, he added, "What took you both so long?"

In a nonchalant manner, but in a guarded voice, Frank explained that he and Joe had stopped to investigate the town of Boonton.

"We thought we'd give you fellows a chance to get settled on the job before we showed up," Joe put in, adding that they had checked in with Mr Losi just before he had left for Bayport earlier that morning. The brothers had learned that no one named Felix was on the work force.

Frank told of the equipment they had brought. "We have got the binoculars, a nylon rope, and a miniature short-wave radio set hidden in a large cinder block under our bunk trailer."

"Good," Tony said with a smile. "The rest of us only brought muscles. And do we need 'em!"

As it grew dark, cool air settled down from the hills and the tired workers drifted away to turn in for the night.

Frank and Joe were billeted in a trailer away from the rest of their pals, with Frank's bunk located above Joe's. Near midnight the Hardys, careful not to awaken their bunk mates, sneaked outside and noiselessly made their way to the neighbouring trailer, housing Angan and Deemer. Voices came from inside.

Joe stood on his brother's shoulders and peered through one of the windows. Angan was sleeping. Deemer was sitting crossed legged-on the floor, playing cards with two men. Willy Teeple looked on sleepily.

As one of the workmen turned his head, Joe ducked out of sight and dropped to the ground. The Hardys pressed close to the metal wall of the trailer and listened intently. The language of the card players was interspersed with many slang words which the boys had never heard before. It certainly was not the jargon of their Bayport High School crowd! The young sleuths made mental notes of the odd expressions.

Pair of bins; oiler; half stamp; clobby joint; long nit; bath in the canal; bice; baron.

"What kind of lingo is that?" Joe whispered.

Suddenly there was a shuffling of feet and Deemer said in a loud voice, "Willy, you be the long nit tomorrow."

"They're breaking up!" Joe muttered. He and Frank hastened to their own bunks and quietly climbed in.

Next morning as the Hardys dressed, Frank whispered to his brother, "Joe, I think I have it solved. I remember Dad speaking about convict lingo, and some of those words last night sounded like jailbird slang."

"Good grief!" Joe exclaimed. "We may be in a hornet's nest of ex-cons."

The working day started early and the Hardys were assigned by Angan to carry planks for the carpenters who were building concrete forms to be used for the bridge's support columns. They spotted their four buddies as they passed by. Frank and Joe also noted that Willy Teeple was nowhere to be seen.

At mid-morning the workmen paused for their coffee break. This gave Frank the chance he had been waiting for. He hastened to his bunk trailer, crawled beneath it, and removed the small radio. Concealing it under his shirt, Frank hurried back to Joe and slipped him the set.

"Quick!" Frank whispered. "Nobody is working on

the bridge now. There's a good hiding place underneath the abutment. Contact Radley and ask him about those strange words.

While Frank stood guard some distance away, Joe nonchalantly ambled over to the bridge. He made sure no one was looking, then ducked underneath, turned on the transmitter, and called Radley in Bayport.

After a few tense minutes of waiting, Joe got through to his father's operative. He spoke rapidly, asking about the odd vocabulary the boys had heard the night before.

"That's con language, all right," Radley said. "Joe, be extra careful!"

Radley translated the words which Joe carefully memorized:

pair of bins	— binoculars
oiler	— soft-soaper
half stamp	— a tramp
clobby joint	— a gambling house
long nit	— a lookout man
bath in the canal	— drown
bice	— two-year prison term
baron	— convict profiting in prison

Joe thanked Radley and signed off. Then he thought in surprise "So that's why Willy's not on the job today— he's lookout for that con bunch."

Joe secreted the short-wave radio in his clothes and started to climb out from under the bridge. Suddenly he stopped short. Nearly concealed behind an empty cement bag were three sticks of dynamite! Joe examined them gingerly. They were not as yet connected with any detonating device.

"So that's next on the gang's list—blow up the bridge!" Joe thought, picking up the sticks. Just then he heard the familiar bird call whistle used by the Hardy boys to warn each other.

Before Joe had a chance to move, Robert Angan scrambled down the slope. He glared angrily at Joe. "So your one of the guys making trouble for us!" Angan said, and snatched the dynamite sticks. "Where'd you get these?"

Joe pleaded innocence, explaining that he had gone under the bridge to cool off during the break and had spotted the explosives there.

"That's a great story," the foreman snorted. He hid the dynamite sticks in his shirt so that the others would not notice them. Then he marched Joe directly to the project shack. Bond Deemer was working on some papers.

Angan produced the explosives. "Caught Jensen here with it."

Deemer was speechless for a moment, then he stormed, "You sneak! You'll go to jail for this."

"But I had nothing to do with this dynamite!" Joe protested. "Remember, I just started work yesterday. Somebody else put these sticks under the bridge."

"Listen Jensen," Angan said, "I had you pegged for a troublemaker the minute you showed up here."

Deemer's anger had receded. He tapped his pencil and looked thoughtfully at Joe. "We can't afford to lose men on this job. Angan. I believe the kid's telling the truth about the explosives."

"Okay," said Angan, pacing nervously. "It's your responsibility, Deemer. But one false move—" he pointed at Joe—"and you're through!"

This time Angan assigned Joe to learn to run a grader machine. "So I can keep you in sight," he said.

Later the foreman approached Frank. "You there, Teller!" he called. "I want you to learn how to handle a pan." He pointed to a huge high-wheeled earth-carrying machine stopped beside the road and Angan called up to the driver, "Yancy, teach this kid how to operate it, then he can spell you."

Frank climbed on to the monster machine, the rubber tyres of which were taller than he. He found Yancy to be a bluff individual, sun-tanned, with bulging arm muscles and a broad face.

The machine started to bounce along, and Yancy readily explained its mechanics to Frank. After the machine had dropped a load of dirt by the side of the road, Yancy turned to his new assistant. "You got an easy job, kid. You must know the baron."

"Who?" Frank could have bitten off his tongue. From that moment on, Yancy said not a word and it was all work and no talk.

Several times Frank tried to start a friendly conversation, but with no luck.

At the end of the day's work, the Hardys met beside the swift-moving stream to wash up.

Frank told his brother of Yancy's clamming up after he had asked who the baron was.

"Do you know where Yancy's bunk is, Joe?"

"Yes, in Deemer's trailer."

"Then I think I'll do a little eavesdropping tonight," Frank said.

An offhand exchange with the other four boys proved that they had uncovered nothing unusual during the day. Late that night Frank sidled up to Yancy's trailer and put his ear close to the door. The voices inside were subdued, but clear enough for the young sleuth to identify them as Yancy's and Deemer's. The boy held his breath and listened intently, noting certain words he was sure were underworld lingo.

Frank heard Deemer mention Joe's name in connection with the discovery of the dynamite. Then Yancy spoke up. "What about this Frank Teller? I thought he was an apple, but he ain't."

A third voice said, "I hear by the grapevine Teller did a bice."

A cold chill went up Frank's spine. So they thought he was an ex-jailbird! "No wonder Yancy figured I knew the baron!" Frank gritted his teeth. "If only I hadn't asked 'who'?"

Suddenly there was a noise nearby. Frank ducked round the trailer and flattened himself against it as a flashlight's beam stabbed the darkness.

· 12 ·

The Protector

FRANK held his breath as the light flashed about near the entrance to the trailer. Then it went off. The door squeaked open and shut.

A voice from inside said, "Oh, it's you Willy. What a layabout! Here, give me the glasses."

"Arkitnay!" retorted Willy Teeple. Frank heard two heavy boots drop to the floor, then all grew silent. Frank waited, but no further talk came from within, so he quietly returned to his own trailer. Inside he whispered to Joe:

"First we have to prove those ex-cons are doing something crooked here. In that case, maybe the police can help us. But we're up against a tough assignment, Joe. Come on. Let's contact Radley again."

The two boys took flashlights and slipped out of the trailer. Joe retrieved the radio set, then the Hardys cautiously made their way into the woods bordering the road.

Once out of sight of the work camp, Frank flicked his light on and off just enough to pick their way through the dense forest. Progress was slow.

"Do you think it's safe to stop now?" asked Joe.

"No. They may have a lookout this close to the trailers."

Stumbling and groping, Frank and Joe plodded on through a stand of pine trees. Finally they came to a small clearing, where the moonlight illuminated a huge boulder. The Hardys dropped to the ground, their backs against the stone.

"Okay," said Frank. "Let's get Radley."

Joe turned on the transmitter, then put in the call to Bayport. No response.

Joe tried again, without results. "Did you check the batteries?" asked Frank.

"There's plenty of juice," his brother replied.

Just then a ham operator came in strong and clear. He asked Joe where he was located.

Joe was polite, but said this was an emergency call and would the ham please sign off.

"As you say. Good luck. Over and out."

"Whew! I hope the cons aren't listening in," said Frank.

"If they are, we're sunk!" declared Joe. He called Radley again. This time a faint reply reached their ears among interference. Joe tuned out some of the static.

"Sam? . . . This is Joe. How's Dad?"

The reply was heartening. Fenton Hardy was improving steadily! "He has intervals of lucidity," Radley reported, "but his memory is foggy."

The operative went on to say that X rays had shown reason for this. "Fenton must have been hit on the back of the neck," Radley said. "The doctors feel that his memory won't be clear for at least a week or so."

"But he will get better!" Joe said tersely.

"Definitely."

With a sigh of relief, Joe passed the radio to Frank, who told Sam, "I've heard some more of those words.

For instance, they called me an apple. What's that?"

"A swindler." Radley chuckled. "They think you're a crook, Frank. That's good!"

"Don't tell Aunt Gertrude!" Frank grinned.

"Got a pencil and paper?" Radley asked. "I can give you a list of prison slang your father compiled."

"Roger."

Joe turned on his flashlight and laid it on the ground. Then, as Sam dictated, he jotted down:

cop a heel	—	to run
tin star	—	country sheriff
torch man	—	safecracker
cheeser	—	a safe easy to open
arkitnay	—	shut up
big note	—	a wealthy man
bindlestiff	—	hobo
in the bing	—	solitary
finger man	—	informer
equalizer	—	gun

Suddenly Radley was cut off.

"Oh—oh, what's up?" Joe fretted.

"Bad atmospheric conditions, probably," Frank said "We'd better get back."

"Okay, swindler," needled Joe. "We have enough words to work on."

They started as quietly as they could. But it was impossible to avoid stepping on twigs which snapped and cracked loudly. Frank used the light sparingly, as a precaution against being spotted.

"Suddenly Joe said, Hey, look!"

Just ahead of them lay a narrow path, which came

to a fork. A right turn would lead them to the camp. The left-hand trail headed in the direction of a mountain ridge. Frank bent down and flashed his light over the ground near the path. Among the matted pine needles was a half-burned safety match.

"Somebody's been using this trail, and more than likely one of the workmen," Frank commented.

"Let's follow it towards the mountain," said Joe.

"Sort of late now."

Joe was not to be dissuaded. "But we might find a good clue."

"Okay, but we can't be long," Frank replied.

At first the path was easy to follow, with the moon providing enough light to guide them. But as the Hardys reached higher ground, a series of switchbacks made the going laborious.

Joe stopped suddenly. "Say, Frank," he whispered, "do you suppose this leads to some kind of lookout spot?"

Instead of answering, Frank seized Joe by the wrist and pulled him behind a pine tree. "I thought I saw something move!" He pointed to an opening between the pines.

"I don't see anything," said Joe.

"Follow me!" Frank ordered. Getting down on all fours, the boys crept across the trail, flattening themselves now and then to listen. They heard a *clink*, like the sound of metal.

Frank skirted round the trees, then stopped at the edge of the opening. Here the pines grew so close together they completely obscured the moonlight.

Joe inched up beside his brother. "It looks like a cave of some kind," he whispered.

Frank nodded, pointing to a stump some thirty feet away, atop which was a box-like object.

The boys lay side by side in the darkness, wondering what to do next. Was someone hiding in the cave? Should they risk entering it? Or should they wait and come back later?

"We have the advantage of surprise," Frank said finally. The boys rose to their feet, then tiptoed forward. Now they could see plainly that the opening was indeed a cave.

"When I shine the light, we'll dash in," Frank said. The flashlight's glare revealed two eyes gleaming at them, as a menacing growl issued from the cave mouth.

"Good grief!" Joe cried out. "A bear!"

As the huge beast lunged from the cave, the Hardys turned and fled. The growls of the bear became fiercer as it crashed through the trees.

Frank and Joe fairly flew on to the trail. Suddenly the bear gave a loud grunt. This was followed by a ferocious thrashing about. Soon the boys realized that the animal was no longer pursuing them. They halted, trembling and out of breath.

"Whew! I thought we were done for," Frank said. "A black bear that size can tear your head off."

The young detectives retraced their steps cautiously to the spot where the bear had stopped. "There he is." Joe pointed, and Frank shone his light on the animal. The boys' jaws dropped in astonishment. The bear was fettered by a long chain, at which he strained towards the box on the stump, two feet away.

"Leapin' lizards!" Frank exclaimed. "That's a bee-hive!"

"What a fiendish set up," said Joe.

The Hardys deduced that someone wanted the trail guarded and had done this by keeping the bear chained in the cave, tantalizing it day and night by a feast of honey just out of reach.

The length of the chain was cunningly contrived, the boys observed. It extended across the trail so that an unsuspecting wayfarer would be frightened out of his wits, or even gravely injured by the voracious bear.

"Bears normally stay out of people's way," Frank remarked, "but this one has a right to hold a grudge against humans."

Making sure to stay clear of the bears' flicking claws, the boys lifted the hive from the stump and heaved it close to the bear, whereupon the animal quickly ripped the hive apart and began to devour the honey.

"Wow! Somebody is going to be surprised!" Joe said, with a chuckle.

They speculated on the reason for the "bear trap," and who was resopnsible, and wondered if it had any connection with their case. The boys started back along the sloping trail. As they descended, the Hardys were startled to hear a man's voice calling:

"Hey, Swede! Teller! Are you there?"

"It's Deemer," Frank whispered. "Let's lie low. We don't want to tip our hand yet."

The Hardys dived behind a thicket and crouched motionless, hardly daring to breath. Suddenly came the sharp crack of gunfire! Bullets whizzed overhead, thudding ominously into the trees. Then it was quiet. Finally the cracking of the twigs came to their ears.

As the sound gradually grew fainter, Joe took a deep breath. "He's leaving. Why do you suppose he shot at us, Frank?"

"He's jittery."

The Hardys made their way cautiously along the trail behind the rifleman. But, again, they were halted by a strange happening. Through the trees a weird rosy pink glow spread over the sky.

"Good grief!" said Joe. "It's not sunrise yet!"

The eerie light gave the black sky an awesome tint.

"This is the spookiest spot I've ever been in," Joe murmured.

"And the most dangerous!" Frank added.

"I'll say! Maybe there's a forest fire!" But Joe's guess proved wrong when the pink light soon vanished and all was dark again.

Mystified, the Hardys went on towards the camp. Every few feet they stopped to listen. The thought of Deemer, perhaps lying in wait to ambush them, caused the boys to break out in a cold sweat. Finally the trailers came into view.

"Look!" said Frank, halting abruptly. In the moonlight they could see Deemer sitting beside the door of their trailer, holding a rifle between his legs.

"Oh, swell!" Joe said in disgust. "How do we get in?"

The boys decided on a decoy action. Joe scooped up a rock and hurled it full force over the trailer. It landed with a thud. Deemer leapt up. Joe tossed another large stone in the same direction.

This time the hiring agent darted out of sight round the trailer.

"Inside, fast!" hissed Frank.

He and Joe sprinted from the trees and slipped into sleeping quarters.

They undressed silently in record time and climbed

into bed. When Frank adjusted his pillow, his hand touched a piece of paper. "Another warning," he thought. By using his flashlight under the cover, Frank read the note. It was from Biff and read:

"Phil's in trouble. Going to be fired. Caught making sketches of D and A."

· 13 ·

Surprise Password

FRANK whispered the message to Joe just before the screen door opened. Deemer stood silhouetted in the doorway, a gun in his hand. He tiptoed over to look at Frank and Joe, who feigned sleep. Joe sat up, as if alarmed.

"Something wrong, Mr Deemer?"

"W-why, I—er—" The hiring boss was clearly flustered. "I thought—er—you'd both gone into the woods and got lost. It's dangerous there, especially at night."

Frank too, sat up and put on a sleepy act. "Mr Deemer, do you usually carry that equalizer?" Joe asked.

Frank turned on his brother and snapped, "Arkitnay!"

Deemer almost dropped the gun and his eyes bulged. He opened his mouth to speak, then evidently thought better of it. Without a word he stalked off to his own trailer.

"We got him worried, anyhow," Joe said with satisfaction.

"Yes, but we'll have to be careful. We're still in the dark as to what his game is."

Despite only a few hours' sleep, Frank and Joe awoke refreshed and keyed up for the sleuthing which lay ahead. At breakfast Frank casually seated himself next to Phil and said, "We heard what happened." Amid the clatter of utensils, Frank instructed his friend, "If you're fired, put on a sad face. Soon as you can, go to Boonton and stay at the Eagle Hotel. We'll get in touch with you there."

Phil nodded. Furthur conversation was impossible because Bond Deemer rose and pounded on the table for attention. "Quiet! Quiet!"

A hush fell over the workmen. Deemer turned to stare at Phil and a sarcastic smile curled his lips. "Rubinow," he said, "if you want to draw pictures, okay. But not here. You're fired!"

With a stricken look, Phil asked, "When?"

"Right now." Deemer pulled a brown envelope from his pocket and flung it at the boy. "Here's your pay. Scram!"

Amid the murmur that arose, Phil, pretending to be stunned, took the envelope and left the trailer.

"He's a layabout, anyway!" Frank said in a voice that could be plainly heard.

Later at the busy construction site, Frank climbed aboard the pan next to Yancy. The motor thundered and growled as the big machine responded to Yancy's touch. It scooped up a huge bucketful of dirt, then trundled off to deposit it by the side of the highway. As they started back for another load, Frank decided to put out a few feelers.

"You think I'm a bindlestiff, eh, Yancy? I figured you to be a finger." Yancy, surprised, jammed on the brake so hard they both nearly flew off the seat. Frank continued. "I'm a torch man, but a tin star caught me on a cheeser. Ain't it the way? Copped a heel but fell flat."

Yancy gave the machine more gas. "You're okay,

Frank and Yancy dived from their seats

kid, but stow the con gab. The baron don't like it. We ain't all in the club."

"What about the local yokels?" Frank parried.

"Most of 'em are okay. They're all scared of Rosy."

"Rosy?" Frank thought fast. "The big fire at night?"

Yancy turned grinning. For a fraction of a second he did not look where he was going. The machine hit a rock projecting from the roadbed and tilted crazily.

"Jump!" Yancy yelled and dived from his seat. Frank followed suit, landing unhurt on the soft shoulder of the road. The vehicle flipped over with the engine racing and wheels twirling madly.

Frank and others workers ran up to Yancy, who had landed on a hard packed surface. He lay moaning, clutching at his right leg. Angan hurried over, looking disgusted. "You're supposed to be an expert!" he growled. "What's the matter with you?"

One of the men arrived with a first aid kit. He stripped the overall from Yancy's leg, and after examining the injury, said, "Afraid it's a bad fracture. We've got to get him to the hospital."

A temporary splint was applied to Yancy's leg. Grimacing with pain, he was placed on a stretcher, which two men slid into the back of a small truck. It eased on to the completed section of the highway and sped away.

Angan turned his attention to Frank. "What happened, Teller?"

Frank shrugged. "Couldn't say."

The foreman scowled. "You guys stick together pretty thick!" he said. "Pick a partner, Teller, and get the derrick to haul up that pan."

Frank looked at his brother. "Hey, Jensen! I could use a squarehead on this job."

With Tony's help, the Hardys directed the crane operator to lift the huge vehicle. It needed a few repairs, which Tony handled with skill. While he worked, the three boys had a chance to confer.

Frank told the others of Yancy's reference to the baron and added, "If we could only get to him!"

"But who is he, and where does he stay?" asked Joe.

Tony had not yet heard any reference to a person called the baron. "I don't think Biff and Chet have, either."

"Quiet!" Frank warned.

A truck hauling rocks had drawn up close to the trio. A brawny man jumped from the cab, motioned Frank aside, and walked him out of earshot of Tony and Joe.

"What's up?" asked Frank.

The truck driver looked him squarely in the eye and said, "Helix."

Two thoughts flashed through Frank's mind: Mr Hardy's mumbled word, which the boys had thought was Felix must instead be helix, meaning a spiral! And the warning received earlier by the Hardys was signed with a three-looped spiral resembling the letter M.

Frank deduced that "helix" must be the gang's password, or at least a special sign used by them.

"Okay." Frank made a spiral loop with his right forefinger and pointed upward. This seemed to satisfy the workman. He beckoned Frank again, moving farther away.

"We got a job to do tonight, Teller."

"A job? On whom?." Frank asked sharply.

"On McGuire. He's been snoopin' around like a dick, so he's gettin' a bath in the canal."

Biff to be drowned? A wave of fear enveloped Frank, but he remained outwardly calm. "How do I know that's true?"

"Listen, If I—Mike Shannon—say so, it's true."

"Okay," Frank said. "McGuire thinks I'm his friend."

"Good. You and the Swede can take care of him at midnight."

Frank trudged back to the pan, his mind in a turmoil. Biff Hooper was the next target of the gang. When Joe and Tony heard of the nefarious plan, they too were horrified.

"We've got to save Biff!" Joe said.

"We will," Frank assured him. "I've got a plan."

It was agreed that Tony would alert Biff later at an opportune moment, give him the plan of action, and warn him to show no surprise or emotion that night when the Hardys came to pick him up.

Outside the trailer after supper, Frank and Joe began a loud argument to provide distraction for Tony to speak with Biff. The Hardys disputed who could heave a rock the farthest. Chet, having been tipped off earlier, joined in the hassle. The three selected a round rock about the weight of a shot and started a contest. The men gathered round, cheering as first one boy then another took turns.

Even Deemer was intrigued. "I can do better than any of you!" he boasted. His put, several inches better than Chet's, spurred others to enter the contest. Tony, after a few hurls, melted away from the crowd and disappeared behind his bunk trailer. Biff, having received the signal from Frank, did the same. A few minutes later the two sauntered back to the contest.

Meanwhile, Chet's practising paid off, and he became champion shot-putter a fraction of an inch over Deemer's best hurl. Everyone cheered, but Angan said acidly, "If you worked as hard with the pick and shovel, Ball, we'd get some work done around here."

"Yes, sir," Chet replied meekly, and laughter drifted among the tall pines.

After sunset, darkness came on quickly and the trees loomed black against the fading daylight. Now the work camp took on a strange, foreboding hush which the Hardys had not experienced before.

Later, finding themselves alone in the trailer washroom, the brothers spoke in whispers.

"I wonder how many of these guys know Biff's due for a bath in the canal," said Joe.

Frank drying his face, muttered through the towel, "Maybe only a few—or maybe more. That's the trouble. We have no idea how many are involved."

In their bunks the two boys passed their time reading magazines. But all the while they had the strange feeling that the others in the trailer were furtively watching them.

At eleven-thirty, Mike Shannon stepped inside and came over to Frank. "Here's the tool you'll need for that job, Teller. In fact, maybe you and Jensen could fix it right now." He slipped a blackjack into Frank's hand and ambled out.

The brothers dressed, noting that the men appeared to be sleeping, undisturbed by Mike's visit.

Five minutes later, the Hardys roused Biff from his bunk. "Hey, McGuire, we got something to show you," said Joe.

"Aw, let me sleep," Biff said, putting on an act.

"Come on, you big lump!"

"Okay, okay." Biff dressed and followed the Hardys outside. As the trio set forth, Frank noticed that Mike and another man were trailing them.

Biff feigned annoyance. "What are you jokers going to show me this time of night?" he asked loudly.

"You'll see. It's down by the water," Joe replied.

The boys made their way through the darkness, guided by the churning sound of the swift-running river. When they reached the edge of the water, the men's footsteps grew louder. "Quick!" said Joe.

Frank drew back the blackjack and made a sweeping motion towards Biff's head. With an anguished cry, Biff keeled over and fell, face down, into the rushing water.

"Boy, what a great act!" Joe whispered gleefully.

But his joy was short lived. As he and Frank started to turn, the two men leaped on them! Each boy was dealt a heavy blow on the head. The Hardys reeled backwards, unconscious, and tumbled into the torrent.

·14·

A Real Sacrifice

FRANK HARDY had the hideous sensation that he was caught in a maelstrom at the bottom of Niagara Falls. Tons of water crushed the air from his lungs, and his chest was constricted by a band of steel.

Then as water swirled about his head, Frank regained consciousness. He was floating on his back, and the tightness round his chest was the strong arm of Biff Hooper.

"Easy, Frank. I got you."

The boy felt himself being grabbed under both arms and pulled up on a stony bank. "You all right?" Biff asked.

At first Frank could hardly speak. His head throbbed and he was half choking from the water he had swallowed. "Joe—Where's Joe?"

"I haven't found him yet. Don't worry. He'll revive and make it to shore."

Frank sat up groggily. "Man oh man, did those crooks double-cross us!" He rubbed his aching head and groaned. "They must've found out who we were! You saved my life, Biff. Thanks! Now we've got to find Joe!"

Frank struggled to his feet and staggered about, trying to regain his equilibrium. Finally his head cleared enough for him to walk without assistance. "We'll follow the shore downstream, Biff."

Pushing their way over jumbled rocks and through tangled brush which grew nearly to the water's edge, the two boys followed the course of the surging stream. Frank stumbled once, but pressed on, his jaw set with determination.

It was half an hour later when the two came to a gentle bend in the river. Silt had washed ashore forming a sandy crescent, and near the middle of it the searchers saw two prone figures. Biff ran ahead, with Frank plodding behind him. Drawing closer, they noticed that the pair were half in, half out of the water.

"Joe!" called Frank. "Is that you, Joe?"

Biff was already kneeling beside one of the figures, when Frank stumbled to his side. The ghostly moonlight revealed the faces of Joe Hardy and Tony Prito!

Tony moaned, stirred slightly, then blinked his eyes. Frank at once applied mouth-to-mouth resuscitation to his brother. Tony, meanwhile, slowly sat up, gasping from ehxaustion.

Finally Joe sucked in a great breath of fresh air. His eyelids fluttered and he smiled wanly at Frank.

"He's okay!" Biff exulted, and set about briskly massaging Joe's ams and legs.

It was not until fifteen minutes later that Joe and Tony felt equal to telling their story. Tony began. He had gone to the Hardys' bunkhouse shortly after the two had left, and from the doorway, had seen Bond Deemer searching through the brothers' belongings.

"Deemer didn't notice me. He exploded when he found your heavy sweaters!" Tony said. "They had your name labels."

"Leapin' lizards!" Joe said weakly. "I know how that happened, Frank."

"So do I. We stuck 'em in at the last second to please Aunt Gertrude and forgot to take the labels off. What goofs!"

Tony reported that he had trailed Deemer, who, furious at the deception, had passed the word along quickly to Mike and another man.

"I couldn't stop them from going after you," said Tony, "so I followed, figuring I could help later, and posted myself downstream a short way."

When he saw the Hardys fall in, Tony had swum to the rescue and reached Joe first. "I spotted Biff grabbing you, Frank."

The Hardys expressed gratitude to their buddies. "We would have been goners without you two," said Joe.

"Which reminds me," Biff said dryly, "the gang probably thinks the three of us are dead."

"And I suppose they've got me pegged," said Tony.

"That leaves Chet alone," said Frank. "He's our only connection now with Deemer and his mob."

The four boys sat on the sand discussing their next move. They all thought that Chet might have a chance to remain unsuspected of being one of the sleuthing team. Should they ask him to stay on the job as their only direct link with the ex-convicts?

"It'll be pretty risky," Joe said. "We'd better leave the decision up to Chet."

Having agreed to this, the boys made their way farther downstream, crossed an old bridge, and edged stealthily back towards the construction camp. Joe had brought a waterproof flashlight, so the quartet had little trouble in finding their way.

Tony, whose bunk was near Chet's, volunteered to rouse him. While the Hardys and Biff waited in the woods, Tony slipped into the trailer. "Keep quiet and come with me," he whispered. "Hurry!"

Befogged with sleep, Chet groped after Tony in the darkness. When they joined the others, Frank and Joe recounted the latest happenings.

The chunky boy was now fully awake. "Zowie, fellows! You sure had a close call!" He shifted uncomfortably. "Guess it'd be awfully dangerous to stay here alone."

"Yes," said Frank. "That's what we are going to ask you about."

"Hmm." Chet drew a deep breath and squared his shoulders.

"Well?" Biff prompted.

"I'll stay!"

"Good boy!" said Joe. "We knew you would."

The plan was to have Chet contact Phil Cohen at the Eagle Hotel in Boonton if anything important developed. "We'll check with him later," said Frank, and added, "Just keep on working as usual, and keep your ears and eyes open."

After handshakes all round, Tony returned with Chet to retrieve the Hardys' radio and binoculars and rope from the cinder block. Chet was about to re-enter his trailer, when Tony said, "Got any food around, Chet?"

"Well, I did stash some away—"

"As usual." Tony chuckled.

Chet disappeared inside and emerged carrying a paper bag. "There's bread and cheese in here," he said. "A midnight snack I was saving. Don't say I never gave you anything!"

"You mean take all of it?"

"Every bit," said Chet. "I better get back."

When Tony told the others of Chet's sacrifice, Joe whistled. "A real pal! Giving up his last bite!"

The four young sleuths pressed deeper and deeper into the woods. Finally they approached the area where the Hardys had seen the eerie rosy light in the sky. There the boys stopped and Frank contacted Radley by radio, giving him a full report.

The operative was stunned to hear what had happened to the Hardys and their friends.

"We're okay now," Frank said. He asked Sam to have the Boonton police keep tabs on Yancy and any visitors at the hospital.

"All right," Radley said. "But from what you tell me, I think we should close in on the mob immediately."

Frank explained that first he wanted to find out who the baron was. "He must be the ringleader," Frank added. "Besides, we have to uncover what's behind the sabotage."

Radley reluctantly agreed to wait, but warned the boys to be extremely careful in their search for the baron. Sam informed the Hardys that their father was improving, but his memory remained unclear. Also, the prisoner Monk Smith had not yet talked.

"We'll keep in touch, Sam," Frank said.

"Over and out.".

"What's next?" asked Biff.

Joe replied promptly. "Get some rest and start out at dawn to find the baron. He had scarcely spoken when a muffled blast in the distance filled the air.

"Dynamite!" Tony cried out.

· 15 ·

A Lofty Lookout

THE blast was followed immediately by a rosy light which spread over the horizon like the aurora borealis. The glow lasted for five minutes, then disappeared.

"That's Rosy," Frank said, recalling what Yancy had told him about the weird light. "I'll bet it's some sort of trick to scare the superstitious hillbillies."

"But why?" queried Biff.

The Hardys both guessed that the strange phenomenon was designed by the criminals to keep the local people in a state of fear, so that they would not interfere with the gang's project.

"Whatever that is," added Joe.

"If their leader can make that kind of magic," Frank went on, "think what would happen to anyone who defected or refused to obey orders."

This line of reasoning interested Tony particularly.

"Then you think Rosy has something to do with the road and bridge construction trouble?"

"Yes," Frank replied, "but the explosion puzzles me. I don't think it sounded like dynamite. I suggest we go on a hunt for Rosy after we get some sleep."

By now the pink hue had died away. The weary foursome selected a sheltered spot, carpeted with pine needles, and flopped down. In a minute all were sleeping soundly.

The sun's rays slanting into his eyes awakened Frank. He roused the others, who stretched and yawned.

"I could have slept all day," said Biff, standing up to flex his muscles.

"Not when we have a date with Rosy," Joe quipped.

Biff came right back. "I wonder if she's as cute as Iola Morton."

Scouting around for a few minutes, Tony found a rivulet of clear spring water. After a refreshing drink, the boys bathed their faces and hands. Next, Chet's gift of grub was divided equally.

When they finished eating, the Hardys decided they should follow the trail which forked up the mountain, since the light seemed to have come from that general direction. Single file, the boys trudged up the slope, circumventing the bear cave.

Suddenly Joe stopped dead in his tracks. "Frank, look at that!" he said pointing.

They all stared at the top of the ridge.

"What do you see?" Biff asked.

"The tallest pine tree right there in the centre. Watch near the top."

A moment later there was a glint as the sun's rays bounced off a bright object.

"Binoculars!" said Frank.

"*Mama mia!*" Tony burst out. "A lookout. The gang must have a hideout nearby."

The boys agreed this would be the most likely place for the gang to post a sentry. A spy, high in the tree, could command a view of the valley and the entire road project. Anybody coming or going on the trail would be in the sweep of vision.

Frank cautioned everyone to walk parallel to the

trail, careful to keep concealed among the trees.

"It might be hard to find the tree when we get there," Frank said, as they neared the ridge. The young sleuths craned their necks but could not see the lookout.

When they reached the summit, the boys glanced in every direction. The boughs grew so thick that it was almost impossible to see the tree-tops in an unbroken line.

"At least," Joe said, "the spy probably can't see us so easily. That's some advantage."

Frank guessed that they might have drifted too far to the south in their climb. "Let's walk north along the ridge," he suggested.

The boys spread out, inspecting one pine after another.

Biff, in the lead, waved wildly, signalling for silence. The others hurreid to where he stood at the base of a towering tree. Biff pointed to an odd-looking cut, slightly higher than his head.

"Good grief!" Joe whispered. "That's the spiral sign."

The carving closely resembled what the Hardys had previously mistaken for an M with three loops.

"This is our tree!" Frank whispered, and looked round at the other side of the trunk. "Oh baby, see what I found!"

A set of spikes, hammered into the tree at regular intervals, provided footholds leading up among the dark branches of the evergreen.

Biff was jubilant. "We've treed the polecat," he said. "Let's climb up and bag him."

"That might not be so easy," Tony said. "We'd probably find ourselves taking a nose dive into the pine needles."

Frank and Joe agreed with Tony. An assault from below could be dangerous. The person perched in the tree had the advantage of height. Also, he might alert the gang through a coded flash of some kind.

"Maybe they'll change lookouts soon," Frank said. "Our only hope is to wait."

The boys posted themselves at various spots within a five yard-radius from the tree and began their vigil. Several times the twittering of birds and the warmth of the sun almost lulled them into drowsiness. Time dragged by.

Frank, rubbing his eyes to stay awake, caught the movement of a small piece of bark floating down from the big pine. He glanced up and saw that the branches far above him were shaking. Their quarry was climbing down. Frank sprang to his feet and signalled to the others. The boys dashed behind a cluster of nearby pines and watched as a pair of long legs came into view, descending the spikes. Then with both arms clinging to the trunk, a tall, gangling youth scrambled to the ground. Simultaneously, the Hardys and their pals leaped from hiding and siezed him.

"Willy Teeple!" Frank cried out. The hillbilly looked half-frightened to death. He squirmed and struggled, but to no avail.

"What were you doing up there?" Frank asked.

"He's the long nit, don't you remember?" Joe put in.

"You—you know about that?" Willy quavered, shaking with fright.

"Of course we do," Tony said.

"Sure," Frank went on, "the helix too, and more."

A look of earnest pleading came into Willy Teeple's

eyes. "Look! You fellows know too much," he said. "Go away and don't come back."

"We're going to stay right here," Joe said, "and get to the bottom of this!"

"Please don't," Willy implored. "Else you'll get the same thing that—that happened to your father!"

The mention of Fenton Hardy electrified the boys.

"What do you know about our father?" Frank snapped.

"Did you have anything to do with what happened to him?" demanded Joe.

Willy shook his head, but would say no more about Mr Hardy.

Both Biff and Tony were all for Willy being turned over to the Boonton police, but the hillbilly begged them not to do this.

"If the boss knows you've captured me, he'll hurt my father," Willy went on.

"Who's your boss—the baron?" Joe prodded.

Willy's face went ashen. "I can't tell you."

"What do you expect?" Frank said. "That we just let you go?"

"I won't fink on you honest!" Willy Teeple said fervently. "I don't want to work for those crooks, but if I say any more, they'll kill me if they find out."

Willy swore again that he would not betray the Hardys and their friends. While Biff kept an armlock on their captive, Frank and Joe stepped aside to discuss the matter.

"Okay," Frank said, stepping forward. "Willy, we'll let you go, but don't say a single word about seeing us."

Joe tried another question. "What about Rosy? Is that part of the gang's scheme?"

Willy, terror in his eyes, remained silent. The boys did find out from him that the trail continued down the other side of the mountain and connected with a narrow road leading to Boonton.

"Fellows, please go away from here. It's awful dangerous," Willy pleaded.

At that moment there was a noise in the underbrush. The four boys ducked out of sight while Willy walked nonchalantly towards the sound. Mike Shannon stepped from the brush. The two merely exchanged nods; then, as Willy Teeple hastened back along the mountain trail, Mike climbed up the spikes of the lookout tree.

"What do we do about this guy?" muttered Biff.

"Nothing yet," said Frank. "We still don't want to alert the baron."

"I think we can trust Willy Teeple," Joe said. "He's in the gang's clutches, for sure."

The four boys set off once more in search of a clue which might lead them to Rosy. As they headed down the opposite slope, Biff, who was in the lead, broke into a trot. Joe was close behind him. Suddenly Biff let out a cry of alarm and disappeared before Joe's eyes!

•16•

Lower than Pigs

JOE checked his speed just in time to keep from falling into a deep pit. Biff lay moaning at the bottom of the hole.

Frank and Tony ran to help Joe pull Biff out.

"Ow! My left ankle! It's broken!"

Frank quickly examined the injury. "It could be, but I think it's only a bad sprain. Here, try to stand." Biff made the attempt, winced, and nearly fell down.

"Somebody pulled a dirty trick," Joe said.

The boys found the freshly dug pit had been covered with boughs and a strip of tar paper, over which pine needles had been scattered.

Frank surmised that they were pretty close to Rosy and that the trap had been placed there to discourage the curious.

After a hurried consultation, it was decided to get Biff back to Bayport as soon as possible.

"We'll have you flown from the Boonton Airport," Joe said. "Phil can go with you. Here, Biff, put an arm round my shoulder."

With Frank and Joe on either side of their injured pal, Biff hobbled as fast as he could. Occasionally Tony relieved each of the Hardys, until they reached the road

117

leading to Boonton. It was gravelly and barely wide enough for two vehicles to pass.

"We might have to wait all day for a lift," Biff said, discouraged. Frank examined the injured ankle once more. It was so swollen that Frank removed the heavy boot. As he did, the sound of wheels drifted from round a bend in the road, and into view came a horse pulling a wagon loaded with pigs.

The driver, obviously a farmer, stopped when the boys hailed him. He was tall and gaunt, showing a thin, weather-beaten face in the shadow of his wide-brimmed hat.

"Going to Boonton?" Joe asked.

"Yep."

"Would you give us a lift? Biff here is injured. Sprained his ankle."

"Ain't room enough."

"Please, Mr—"

"Teeple's the name." The man tilted his hat and jerked a thumb towards his pigs. "I'm going to market. Got a full load."

Frank tried a long shot. "Are you Willy Teeple's father?"

The question caught the man by surprise. "You know my son?"

"Sure he works for the baron!"

"You in that gang too?" the farmer asked, frightened, and Frank saw he was about to put the whip to the horse.

"Wait, Mr Teeple. No, we don't work for the baron, but we heard about him, on the road job. Do you know who the baron is, and where he hides out?"

The farmer grew agitated. "All I can say is the baron's

a bad man. I don't know what he's done to my Willy. But terrible things have been happening. Okay, the three of you get in the back with the pigs. I'll take the injured lad up front with me."

Frank, Joe, and Tony pushed Biff up on to the seat beside Willy's father. Then they jumped into the back with the pigs, and the wagon started towards Boonton.

"What are you boys doing here?" the farmer asked. "It's dangerous."

"Willy told us that," Frank said. "We're looking for Rosy."

"The devil himself makes that fire!" the farmer exclaimed. On further questioning, he told the boys that several people who ventured near it had vanished. "Including a detective!"

Before Frank could ask another question, a jeep appeared over the brow of a rolling hill, a mile away. Joe whipped the binoculars to his eyes.

"Here comes trouble. Four rough-looking customers and I'll bet they're the baron's men."

"We'll have to hide among the pigs," Frank said. He grabbed Biff by the shoulders and pulled him into the back of the wagon. Then the four companions lay flat with the pigs snorting and grunting and stepping on them with their cloven hoofs.

"This isn't exactly a perfume factory," Joe remarked.

"Quiet," Frank whispered. "Here comes the car."

With screeching brakes, the jeep came to a stop, alongside the farmer's wagon.

"Hey, you! We're looking for four guys. Have you seen 'em?"

"What you say?"

"We're looking for four of our road crew. They've stolen the payroll!"

"Hey what?"

"Oh, he's deaf," one of the men growled. "Let's go."

The jeep roared off, and when it was out of sight, the youths crawled from under the pigs.

"Thanks, Mr Teeple!" Frank said. "That was a close call for us. And we're not thieves."

"I know it."

The wagon crossed a small brook and stopped so that the boys could wash and bathe Biff's swollen ankle in the cold water. When they finally arrived at the airport, the Hardys and their pals thanked the farmer.

"Don't worry, Mr Teeple," Frank said. "Your son is okay. We're going to try to help him! But don't say a word about this to anybody."

The farmer promised and the hitch-hikers got out, assisting Biff gingerly into the terminal building. Joe immediately phoned Phil, asking him to check out of the hotel and hurry to the airport. Then the starved boys went to the lunch counter.

By the time they had finished three hamburgers apiece, Phil Cohen stepped out of a taxi and ran to greet them. After hearing their story, he said, "I've got some news, too."

Phil reported spying on four suspicious men staying at his hotel. "I heard them giving the password 'helix' to the bellman," he said, and pulled a sketch from his pocket. It showed the faces of the four men.

"I think they're the ones who were in the jeep," said Joe. He took the sketch for future reference.

When Phil heard he was to accompany Biff back to

Bayport, he asked, "But what do we do for money?"

"Fly now, pay later." Frank chuckled, and hurried away to convince a charter pilot that Radley would pay the bill at Bayport.

After the two boys had flown off, Frank, Joe, and Tony went directly to the Boonton police station. There they inquired whether Yancy had any visitors at the hospital. A lieutenant named Murphy reported that Yancy had had only one visitor—a seedy fellow who looked harmless enough. "Claimed to be a distant cousin."

"Did you put a tail on him?" asked Tony.

Murphy said a patrolman had shadowed the man as far as a shack at the outskirts of Boonton. "It convinced us that he was just a drifter," Murphy continued, "so we didn't bother any further."

The boys thanked the officer, got directions to the shack, and hastened to find it. It was located not far from the town dump, and was constructed of old planks and wooden packing cases. The makeshift roof of corrugated iron, was full of holes.

The trio approached the rickety door of the windowless shelter. Frank listened. Silence. He opened it quietly and the three stepped inside.

"This isn't exactly the Waldorf-Astoria," Tony said with a chuckle. The shack was littered with empty bottles, tin cans, and stacks of old newspapers.

Frank and Joe immediately poked about the debris, looking for a clue to the mystery man. On the floor, sticking out from under a mouldy mattress, was the handle of a briefcase. As Joe bent down to reach for it, footsteps sounded outside.

"He's coming back," Frank whispered. "Duck!"

The boys hid behind a stack of cartons and listened. The footsteps came closer, then circled the shack. Finally the door opened slowly.

"Oh boy!" a childish voice rang out. "He's not here today either."

"Now we can play the detective club again," a second voice chimed in.

Frank, Joe, and Tony stepped out from behind the boxes to see the two young boys peering inside. They cried out with fright, turned and fled.

"Come back here," Joe called. "We're not going to hurt you!"

The youngsters stopped, then hesitantly returned. "You aren't robbers or anything?" asked the older one, who was about ten.

"Of course not," said Joe. "Say, what are your names?"

The older boy was Andy Pulaski; the other, three years younger, was Rick. "We're brothers and we live in Church Street," declared Andy. He said they often came to the shack to play, but a rough-looking man had scared them away several times.

"He's a tramp!" Rick said, nodding his head vigorously. "I can tell, 'cause he doesn't shave."

"Well you can play here all you want," said Frank. He reached down and pulled the briefcase from under the mattress. Then, leaving the boys to their fun, the young sleuths hastened away.

In the seclusion of a grove of trees, Frank and Joe stopped to examine the briefcase, while Tony looked on.

Both sides were scorched and charred, and the place

where initials would normally be imprinted was covered with dried mud.

Frank took out his knife and scraped away the crusty dirt. The initials showed up clearly—F. H.!

· 17 ·

Dangerous Terrain

"DAD'S briefcase!" Joe exclaimed. He opened it and looked inside. The case was empty, except for a gritty white substance at the bottom.

"Limestone!" Frank said. "Come on, fellows."

On the double, he led them back to the shack where the two Pulaski youngsters were playing. Frank asked more questions about the man who had chased them away, but the children were vague in their discriptions.

"When he yelled 'Scram,' Rick and I just ran," Andy said.

"He scared me," Rick added. "I didn't look back."

Joe produced the sketches which Phil Cohen had made. "Did that fellow look like any of these?" he asked.

The children looked at the sketches and shook their heads.

"Well, if he comes back and chases you away again," Frank said, "please tell us. We'll be staying at the Eagle Hotel. Ask for Frank, Joe, or Tony."

"Are you detectives?" asked Andy.

"Sort of," said Joe.

"Gee, we'd like to know how to be real detectives," said Rick. "Will you show us someday?"

"Maybe," Joe replied. "See you later."

Leaving the boys, Frank, Joe and Tony made their way back to town. First, they stopped at the police station to report to Lieutenant Murphy what they had found and to leave the briefcase there for safekeeping.

The lieutenant made a note of their investigation, saying he would be on the lookout for the vagrant. He added, "Maybe the old geezer found your father's briefcase somewhere. Doesn't mean he stole it."

Frank agreed that they should not jump to conclusions, but said he still believed that the shack dweller must be considered a suspect.

"And what about this light in the sky called Rosy?" Joe asked.

"Oh, that," Murphy said with a shrug. "I've never seen it myself. Who knows what to believe?" Chuckling, he added, "These hill folks tell some awful tall tales."

Frank told the police officer that they would be staying at the Eagle Hotel, in case any new leads turned up.

The boys went directly to the hotel, located two blocks from the station house. It was an old frame building with a small lobby. The boys registered as Frank Brown, Joe Jones, and Tony Wilson and paid in advance for one night's lodging.

"No bags?" the clerk asked.

"We're travelling light," Frank replied.

The clerk summoned the bellman, a stoop-shouldered and shifty-eyed individual. He led the boys to a room on the first floor, in which there were twin beds and a bunk. After showing them the bath, the man left.

Meanwhile, the three boys flopped onto their beds.

But the next instant Frank jumped up and said, "There's something I forgot to ask Murphy." He went to the telephone and had a call put through to the lieutenant. Frank questioned him about limestone deposits in the area. He was told that there undoubtedly were some in the caves and a natural bridge deep in the woods.

"But nobody goes there," the officer said.

"Why?"

"Dangerous terrain."

Frank was about to quiz Murphy further, when he heard breathing on the line. Quickly he thanked the lieutenant and hung up.

"An eavesdropper!" Frank said.

"The bellman, I'll bet," Tony exclaimed. "Phil warned us about him."

Joe bolted the door, while Frank switched on an antique radio which stood on the bureau. A shrill jazz tune welled up.

"Nobody can overhear us now," Tony said. "Where do we go from here, fellows?"

"Find Rosy," Frank said promptly. "If we do, I'm convinced we'll also find the baron. My guess is he's behind that black magic."

"First I want a good hot bath," Joe said, stripping off his clothes.

He was in and out of the tub quickly. Tony followed. By the time Frank had finished towelling himself and stepped back into the bedroom, both Joe and Tony were sleeping soundly. Frank, too, stretched out, and despite the late-afternoon sunlight streaming in, he fell asleep as soon as his head touched the pillow.

The boys wakened to find it dark outside. Tony

Joe snatched up the sheet of paper

checked his watch. "Nine-thirty! Did we need that sleep!" he said.

"And I could use some chow, too," Joe declared.

They dressed and were about to leave, when Frank suggested he and Joe take along the short wave, the binoculars, and the rope. "Just in case somebody breaks in," he said.

As the boys walked through the lobby, they noticed the bellman, his head tilted forward, apparently dozing. He did not stir as the trio passed. They found a restaurant several doors from the hotel, and had a hearty, though inexpensive meal.

"How's our money holding out?" Joe asked as Frank paid the bill.

"For payroll robbers we're pretty broke," Frank quipped, then added seriously, "It's time we phoned Radley."

On the street once more, the sleuths found a public booth and Frank called Sam's number, reversing the charges. Radley was not at home, but his wife accepted the call. She said that her husband had gone to the airport and met Biff and Phil. An examination by a doctor showed that Biff had, indeed, suffered a severe sprain.

Mrs Radley reported that Mr Hardy continued to gain strength, but it would take time to overcome his lapse of memory.

"Your mother and Aunt Gertrude are fine," Mrs Radley added. "Any message for them?"

"Tell them we're okay," Frank replied. "Thanks, and good night, Mrs Radley."

Back at the hotel, the boys went quietly to their room. Frank turned the key, opened the door, stepped inside, and switched on the light. As he did, something white appeared from under the connecting door of the adjoining room.

Joe leaped to snatch it up. "A message!" he said, unfolding the sheet of paper. He read it aloud:

" 'Get out! This is your last warning!' And signed 'the baron'!" Joe held out the paper and they all saw beneath the name the now-familiar spiral sign.

Before the Hardys could stop him, Tony rushed out into the hall. In two strides he reached the adjoining room and tried the door. It was not locked, and he pushed it open. The room was pitch-dark. The light from the hallway failed to show any occupant. Tony slipped inside and felt for the light switch, but before his fingers could reach it, the door suddenly slammed shut. A brass-knuckled fist crashed against the side of his head and he went down in a heap!

A moment later the Hardys reached the closed door and pushed against it.

"Something's propped against the other side," Joe said.

He and Frank put their shoulders against the door and shoved it open enough for Frank to squeeze inside. He found the switch and flicked on the light. Frank gasped. Tony lay unconscious behind the door!

Frank ran to the open window, which opened on to a fire escape. Nobody there. He tried the connecting door to their room. Locked. Whoever delivered the note and the knockout blow had made a neat getaway.

The Hardys carried Tony back into their room, where he was revived with a cold compress. He stood up shakily.

"Whoo!" he said. "I'm—dizzy."

"We'd better get a doctor," said Joe. "You may have concussion."

Frank decided to use a telephone outside the hotel to call a doctor and to report the attack to the police. He returned saying that a Dr Jones was on his way.

All the boys were relieved when the examination indicated that Tony needed only a few days' complete rest before resuming normal activity. When the doctor had left, the young detectives were in a quandary as to where Tony might stay.

"It better be some place unknown to the baron," Frank remarked.

"You're right," said Joe. "That gang leader is picking us off one by one—divide and conquer."

"I've got an idea," Frank said. "How about those two kids we met at the shack?"

"Good grief," Tony moaned. "I don't want to stay in that dump!"

"No, not there," Frank went on. "Remember Andy and Rick want to be detectives? Maybe their mother would put you up until you feel better. Meanwhile, Joe and I will look for Rosy and the baron."

The Hardys thought they should leave the hotel at once. "One attack's enough," said Joe.

Tony was able to navigate with the Hardys' help, so the boys took their belongings and went downstairs. Nobody was in sight, not even the desk clerk.

Outside, they soon got a taxi and climbed in. The driver was familiar with Church Street and knew where the Pulaski brothers lived. He let the boys off in front of a modest, neat-looking house.

Frank rang the doorbell. A tall, lean man answered. "Mr Pulaski? Sorry to bother you so late."

"Yes. What can I do for you fellows?"

Quickly Frank explained about Tony, without giving specific details of the mystery. He did say that he and his brother Joe were working on an important case.

"We met your sons Andy and Rick," Frank went on, smiling. "They told us they'd like to be detectives, so we thought maybe Tony could give them some pointers in exchange for you giving him shelter. Of course we'll pay you—"

Mr Pulaski broke in. "Don't worry about that. Be glad to help you out. Come on inside. My wife's right smart 'bout takin' care of sick folk."

Mrs Pulaski proved to be a cheerful, kindly woman. "We've got a spare room all ready," she told Tony. "Make yourself at home."

"Thanks, ma'am. That's swell."

Just then footsteps sounded on the stairway, and Andy and Rick in pyjamas scampered joyfully into the living-room.

"I knew you'd all come back!" Ricky said. " 'Cause you're going to show us how to be detectives."

When they heard that Tony was to stay for a few days the youngsters were overjoyed. Frank now cautioned the family, "We'd appreciate it if nobody else knows he's here."

The Pulaskis all readily agreed, eager to assist the young sleuths in the mystery. Sure that Tony was in good hands, Frank and Joe thanked the family and left. They walked through Boonton, found the road over which they had ridden in Teeple's wagon, and began to hike back towards the wilderness. The night was cool and the moonlight bathed the countryside.

Three miles out of town a small truck rumbled up behind them and the boys thumbed a ride. The driver, an affable young man, took them to the place where they had met Mr Teeple and the Hardys hopped out.

Using their flashlights, they found the trail over the ridge and made their way back to the dense woods. The boys kept a constant alert for the rosy glow, but the sky remained dark.

"Guess Rosy's taken the night off," Joe said, as they carefully skirted the pit into which Biff had fallen. The trap had not been reset.

"What do you make of that, Frank?"

"They think we've cleared out."

"But what about other snoopers?"

"Oh, I guess the baron thinks he has everybody else under control and scared. Just as well for us."

The boys continued to a spot not far from the trailers. There they stopped to rest.

"As soon as possible, let's talk to Chet. Maybe he's found new evidence," said Frank.

The loud chirping of birds awakened the Hardys to a bright, hot morning. Nearby was a tall tree which they climbed for a better view of the road-building operation. Activity was already under way, as engines coughed and the various crews began their day's work.

Joe pressed the binoculars to his eyes. "I see Chet!" he said. "Take a look."

Chet was shovelling dirt by the roadside, not far from the bridge. The Hardys shinned down the tree, then advancing cautiously on stomachs and elbows, edged closer for a better look. Now Frank had the glasses trained on Chet's face. The stout boy kept glancing at the bridge, frowning. Finally he edged his way steadily to the span.

Suddenly Frank turned to his brother. "Joe, something's up!"

· 18 ·

A Shot-put Blast

OBLIVIOUS of the fact that Frank and Joe were watching him, Chet Morton scrambled down the river bank and peered under the partially completed bridge. The round black object lying there intrigued him.

It appeared to be a kerosene flare, the kind which workmen use at night to warn passers-by of construction dangers. But the wick was not lighted. And wasn't it odd, Chet thought, that the bridge crew had not yet appeared?

Chet glanced at his watch. It was quarter past seven. Angan was always furious if work did not start at seven sharp. Chet looked up. There was the foreman himself, starting down the bank towards him.

"Maybe he knows about this flare," Chet thought, and advanced to pick up the black object. He bent down and lifted it.

Tick-tick-tick-tick!

Like a bolt of lightning, the horrible truth struck Chet. This was no flare. It was a time bomb!

Chet was so paralysed with fear that he could not drop the menacing black ball. Instead, he ran towards Angan with it.

"Mr Angan! Mr Angan!"

"What you got there?"

"A b-b-bomb!"

Angan froze like a statue. "A bomb! Get rid of it!"

Chet wheeled about and assumed his best shot-putting stance. And, with the ticking loud in his ear, he let the object fly! It was a record-shattering heave, sailing high over the bridge and landing downstream some fifty feet. Before the swirling current carried the missile twenty more feet, the air was rent by a deafening explosion. Rocks and debris shot high into the air, falling back into the water like giant hailstones. But the bridge was not damaged.

Chet Morton quaked with shock. Speechless, he faced the foreman.

Angan roared, "Where'd you get that bomb?"

"I—I found it under the bridge."

"You're a liar! Same as Joe Jensen!" Angan lunged to grasp Chet, but the stout boy darted out of his way.

When necessary, Chet could move swiftly despite his weight and he sprinted up the riverbank towards the woods bordering the road construction.

"Stop!" the foreman cried out, in hot pursuit. "Stop, or I'll have you arrested!"

Chet paid no heed. The Hardys' faithful pal bull-dozed through a thicket close to where Frank and Joe were hiding. Muttering dire threats, Angan charged after him. But his chase ended in a dull thud as he hit the ground with Joe Hardy's arm clamped around his legs.

The foreman tried to rise, only to be pinned by Frank. Chet had glanced over his shoulder to see what the commotion was about. He retraced his steps, a look of surprise and gratitude on his round, perspiring face.

"Where—where'd you guys come from?"

"Explain later!" Frank replied. "Chet, you saved the bridge!"

"And thousands of dollars for Mr Prito," Joe added.

"Let me up!" Angan spluttered. He strained and tried to kick, but the Hardys held him down firmly.

"Chet, grab that vine!" Frank commanded.

Chet pulled up a stout green tendril and handed it over. Frank and Joe deftly made loops and secured Angan's hands and feet.

"I'll get you for this!" he threatened.

"The gang's already tried that!" Joe retorted. "Are you in with them too?"

Without waiting for an answer, they left their trussed-up captive and melted into the woods.

Frank and Joe were unstinting in their praise for Chet. The stout boy beamed with pride. "That shot-putting stuff came in handy, eh?"

"Sure did," Joe remarked. "I think you broke the world record, Chet!"

The Hardys headed for the mountain trail, and as they pushed on through the woods, they briefed Chet on their adventures and what had happened to Phil, Biff, and Tony. In turn, Chet told the brothers what new information he had learned.

"Word got around," he said, "that anybody who stepped out of line would be treated like you three guys. And they were sore when Tony disappeared."

"Is the whole crew made up of ex-jailbirds?" asked Frank.

Chet replied that from what he had overheard, he judged only a handful of the men worked for the gang. "But they're enough to keep the job slowed down to scare the other workers."

"If only we knew which ones are sabotaging the bridge," Frank said.

Chet expressed the belief that despite Angan's bad temper, he was loyal to the Prito company.

"Deemer's a big wheel in the gang," the chunky boy went on. "He was really burned up when you fellows let the bear eat the honey."

"So he knows we did that," Joe remarked. "Wonder if that trap was his idea."

"Does Deemer know he didn't succeed in drowning us?" Frank asked.

Chet bobbed his head. "They picked up your tracks in the woods, and I heard last night you were in Boonton."

"The baron has a regular spy network," Frank observed. He and Joe were sure that the bellman had reported the Hardys' presence. Chet had not learned anything about the baron's identity, or the secret of Rosy.

"You did some swell detective work, though," Joe said.

The stout boy grinned. "I just eat and listen."

"Which reminds me—it's nearly lunchtime," Frank said, "and our stock is nil."

"Fear not," said Chet. He reached into his bulging shirt pockets and produced three sandwiches. "I was saving these for coffee break, minus the coffee."

The boys stopped near the brook, ate the sandwiches, and had a refreshing drink of cold, clear water. Afterwards, the Hardys renewed their quest for Rosy. With Chet, they set forth up the mountain trail, giving the bear's cave a wide berth. This time the boys did not cross the ridge, deciding instead to search the terrain south of the trail.

It was almost dusk when the trio paused to rest near a patch of wild blackberries, which they ate with zest.

"We'd better find a good place to camp for the night," Frank said.

All three scouted about until Chet came upon a shaded glen. Alongside it was a waterfall, which dropped in a foaming arch some ten feet into a deep, gurgling stream.

The boys cut branches for a lean-to, had supper of more berries, then settled back to watch for the rosy light in the darkening sky. Because all were weary from the day's tramp, the young sleuths took turns standing watch. Joe's turn was ten until midnight. He sat with his back against a tree, desperately trying to keep his eyes open until the stroke of twelve. Once his chin bobbed against his chest, and he opened his eyes with a start. The night sky seemed brighter.

"Frank! Chet!" Suddenly the pink light mushroomed into the sky, with a brilliance which made the boys gasp. "Rosy!"

"Leapin' lizards!" Joe exclaimed. "It's close by!"

Excitedly the trio scrambled out of the glen in the direction of the light. They crossed the stream and climbed to the top of a small knoll. The Hardys and Chet looked down in amazement at the scene below.

Out of a depression in the ground issued a stream of fire. Around it moved the figures of several men, their forms silhouetted against the glow.

"Good grief! What'll we do?" Chet whispered.

"Get out of sight!" Frank commanded. "The light's shining on us, too, you know."

The boys ducked for cover, raising their heads now and again above the rise to take in the awesome sight.

Suddenly the flame diminished and disappeared.

"Let's go back," Frank said. "If we're caught prowling around here now, we've had it!"

Despite their weariness, the Hardys slept little the rest of the night, wondering what the significance of their discovery was. Would it give them the solution to the mystery they had come to solve?

As soon as dawn tinged the horizon, the trio set off again. They advanced over the knoll and looked down at the spot where the great flame had been. There they saw a charred area, thirty feet in diameter. In the centre of it, a black pipe protruded from the ground.

Chet Morton sniffed. "I smell gas!"

"Me, too," said Joe.

The same thought dawned on all three boys at the same time. *A gas well!*

"Jeepers! Why didn't we think of that!" Joe's exclamation was punctuated by the sound of rifle-shots. Bullets thudded into trees near the boys.

"Run for it!" Frank yelled.

As he and the others turned to flee, Mike Shannon and another man raced up the knoll.

"Stop, or we'll shoot!" Shannon ordered. But the Hardys and Chet kept going.

They swerved sharply and plunged through a thicket. Their skin was scratched and their clothes torn by the brambles, but the barrier delayed their pursuers. More bullets ripped the twigs perilously close to the boys' heads.

"They'll pick up our trail again," Joe muttered. "We'd better find a place to hide!"

"The waterfall!" Frank said. "We can hide behind it!"

Reaching the stream, the boys splashed into the water and made their way towards the churning falls. They burst through the curtain of water and stood chest-high in the swirling eddies.

"What'll we do if they look behind the falls?" Chet asked.

"Duck under," Joe said, "and hold our breath."

Just then two dark forms appeared on the other side of the opaque watery screen.

"Down!" Frank commanded.

· 19 ·

The Spiral Bridge

EACH boy sucked in a chestful of air and sank beneath the surface. How long could they hold out? All their athletic training came into play at this crucial moment. Thirty seconds. Forty-five. One minute! Their lungs ached for oxygen.

Frank swam to the rocky wall behind the cascade. He had to surface! Coming up slowly, he scanned the watery chamber. Chet and Joe appeared at the same time.

"We fooled them!" Joe whispered.

"You think they'll look for us here?" Chet asked.

The Hardys could not answer with certainty, but at least the shadowy shapes could not be seen through the tumbling screens of water.

"Maybe we ought to wait here a while," Chet suggested.

"Not too long," Frank said. "If Mike Shannon and his pal think we've escaped, now's our chance to turn the tables and trail them."

"That's right," Joe agreed. "They might lead us right to the baron's hideout."

The three sleuths let a few more minutes elapse, then Joe volunteered to be first out of the waterfall hideaway. He swam underwater, surfaced, and quickly reported back to the others that Shannon and his crony were nowhere in sight. The boys swam out cautiously, climbed out of the stream, and wrung the water from their clothes.

"Lucky it's a hot day," said Joe. "Won't take long to dry off."

Their field glasses were soggy but not damaged, and the short-wave, which Joe carried, was protected by a waterproof pouch.

The boys plan was to fan out in order to pick up the trail of their erstwhile pursuers. The Hardys' bird whistle would be the signal if anyone came across the trail. The trio proceeded, still bearing south.

It was Frank who found the tracks made by the two men. Broken twigs and trampled underbrush told him that their enemies apparently had made no effort to conceal their route. Frank gave the whistle. Joe and Chet joined him on the run.

"Remember," Frank said, "these men are armed. They'll really let us have it if they spot us again. We'll trail them, but be careful!"

It took only a short time for the boys to catch sight of their quarry. Shannon and his partner were climbing over a jagged outcrop on a steep, rocky slope. The ground ahead was rough and uneven, and the Hardys recalled Lieutenant Murphy's statement about dangerous terrain.

The boys waited until the men had disappeared over the crest of the hill.

"Okay," whispered Frank. "Let's go."

Exercising the utmost stealth, the boys advanced to the slope. Loose stones and shale underfoot made the ascent difficult. A false step could mean a landslide, or painful fall. Finally the Hardys and Chet reached the top. Below was a long valley, creased by a placid stream. Spanning this was a natural bridge of great beauty, resembling a noble arch.

The men were just nearing the span. Suddenly they vanished!

"They didn't go under the bridge or round it!" Chet said.

Frank and Joe studied the formation through the binoculars. It was obviously composed of limestone, about fifteen feet thick. The left side of the bridge jutted out from high ground, then curved gracefully to the right, down amid a jumble of boulders at the level of the brook about seven yards from the shore.

Crawling from bush to bush, the boys drew closer to the bridge. Frank stopped to study it again with the field glasses. Now he saw that in the centre of the arch on the underside, there was an opening the size of a manhole, through which water dripped into the stream below.

"Chet, you stand as a lookout," Frank said, "while Joe and I scout around the bridge. These crooks must have a hideout nearby. If you see anyone coming, give the bird whistle."

Chet concealed himself behind a thicket, while the Hardys darted from bush to tree as they moved towards the lower side of the natural bridge. There they examined the crevices among the boulders, but did not find an opening.

Since there was no warning from Chet, Frank and Joe boldly struck across the shallow water and climbed the slope to the top of the bridge. Carefully they walked on to the flat surface.

"Look at this." Joe pointed to a small trickle of water which seemingly vanished into a small hole in the rock.

"That explains it!"

"Explains what?"

"The water coming out of that hole underneath," Frank replied. He reasoned that the tiny rivulet, over thousands and thousands of years, had cut into the limestone bridge and gouged its way out underneath.

Joe snapped his fingers. "Frank!" he said quietly. "Do you suppose this whole bridge could be hollowed out by water erosion?"

Frank shrugged. "Could very well be."

The boys returned to Chet and told him what they had found.

"What a great tourist attraction!" Chet declared. "Boy, I'd like to have the concession for a lemonade and hot-dog stand!"

"No doubt." Joe groaned. "Chet, you would have to talk about food when we haven't a crumb to eat!"

"Cut the chatter," Frank warned. "Those crooks might be listening to us right now." In low tones he urged that they scour every inch of the ground around the natural bridge. "Mike and the other man didn't just vanish by magic!"

It took until late afternoon before Joe stumbled upon a clue. He noted that a number of branches had been freshly cut from a willow tree.

"You think they were used for camouflage, Frank?" Joe asked.

"That's my guess," Frank said. "They're hiding something."

"Come on. We've got to find it," Joe said excitedly. The rays of the sinking sun were filtering through the treetops, casting an oblique light on the forest floor. It was then that a glint caught the searcher's eyes. It showed through what appeared to be a thicket, but on closer examination the Hardys found a cleverly rigged bower of willow boughs.

Tensely the boys parted the greenery and peered into the depths. *The glint shone from the steering wheel of a jeep!* "The same jeep we saw coming from Boonton!" Joe exclaimed.

The boys found that the vehicle bore a licence number, but otherwise no identification. The Hardys, however, noted that the hiding place was close to the right-hand base of the natural bridge, with the car facing the rock pile.

The trio posted themselves near the camouflage for an hour, but nobody appeared. Soon it began to grow dark and the boys retreated downstream to observe the bridge. As darkness fell, Chet suddenly pointed to the underside of the span. "Frank! Joe!" he said excitedly. "There's a light coming from that hole!"

"Somebody's inside!" Frank turned to his brother. "Joe, your guess about erosion really hit the mark! The bridge itself is the gang's hideout!"

But how to get inside? Frank finally came up with a plan. "There must be an opening among those boulders. Joe, you and Chet look again. I'll stand guard here."

Joe left the binoculars, a torch, and the radio with Frank. Also the nylon rope, which he had carried looped from his belt.

The light from the rising full moon helped to guide Chet and Joe to the other side of the brook and the rocky base of the arch.

This time even the surface of each boulder was examined carefully. One after another proved to be hard and firm, with no hint of a possible crevice entrance-way.

Suddenly Chet beckoned excitedly to Joe, who scrambled over.

"Look!" Chet whispered. He pointed to a yawning hole near the bottom of a huge boulder. "I can just squeeze through it!"

Joe put his ear to the opening. The sound of men's voices echoed dimly from inside.

"Let's get Frank!" Chet whispered.

"Wait," Joe whispered. "If we can case this layout, it'll be a big help to the police."

Reluctantly Chet agreed. "Lead on," he said, with a resigned sigh.

The narrow opening quickly gave way to a tunnel which was head high. Joe and Chet stood up and listened. When their eyes became accustomed to the dimness, the boys felt their way upwards along what proved to be a series of looping curves.

A thought struck Joe. "Sure!" he said aloud. "This passage is like a spiral! That explains the helix password. Dad must have discovered this natural bridge just before he was captured!"

Chet opened his mouth to reply, but never did. Suddenly two men sprang towards them from tall niches on either side of the rock wall.

Joe and Chet, caught off balance, struggled violently, but in vain. Ropes bound their arms to their sides and they were pushed roughly along through the spiral interior. Here and there, kerosene lanterns, fastened to the wall, lighted the sinister faces of their captors. Neither was familiar to the boys. "We got you pests for good this time!" snarled one. "Your luck's run out."

"It sure has, Pete," the other chortled.

By now they were at the top of the arch where the tunnel levelled off. The captive sleuths were shunted into a small side chamber, carved out of solid rock. The light from several lanterns showed the place to be a veritable arsenal, with weapons of all types hanging on the walls, and around a rough hewn-table in the centre sat four men—the same men who had been riding in the jeep the other day.

Another man, tall and gaunt-faced, stood lounging in the shadows against the far wall. When he came forward into the light, Joe's jaw dropped and he stared at the man in utter disbelief.

"Mortimer Prince!" The vagrant Frank and Joe had met in New York!

As Joe watched, half-dazed, Mortimer Prince moved to the head of the table and sat down. The thug called Pete stepped up and addressed him with an air of great self-satisfaction.

"We got the Hardy boys. What'll we do with them, Baron?"

· 20 ·

Swinging Tactics

JOE blinked in astonishment. Mortimer Prince was the baron! The gang leader rose from the table, his face contorted in fury.

"Fools!" Prince stormed at the two henchmen. "You only got Joe Hardy. This fat boy is not Frank!"

Pete looked frightened. "Ferd and I thought we had 'em both." He pointed to Chet. "You sure he ain't Frank Hardy?"

"I know the Hardys!" the baron shouted. "Get going and nab Frank!"

Ferd and Pete scurried out of the rock-hewn chamber. In an undertone, Joe rapidly told Chet that the baron was the tramp that he and Frank had encountered in Manhattan. "Shut up, you two!" the baron ordered.

"Who are you, anyway?" Joe asked boldly. "And what kind of racket are you up to?"

"Never mind. It's enough for you to know that I've outsmarted Fenton Hardy and his sons!"

"You're the one who nearly killed my father!" Joe said angrily. "Why?"

The baron's eyes held a cruel glint. "That old man of yours sent me up the river twice!"

One of Prince's henchmen said menacingly, "Nobody can do that to the baron. It means curtains!"

Chet went white as a sheet, and Joe felt a tingle of fear up his spine. *If Frank could only get away!* Meanwhile, Joe decided to try stalling for time.

"Those ex-cons working for you now," he said, "aren't following your orders to sabotage the road construction just for laughs."

"That's right." The baron was obviously pleased with himself. "Once you and your nosey pals are out of the way, I'll put kibosh on Prito's job permanently."

Chet found his voice. "You'll never get away with it."

"Ha-ha! listen to fatso!" came Mike Shannon's sneering voice as he entered. "This time you punks are all washed up."

Joe ignored him and shot another question at the baron. "Are you trying to prevent the road from being built because of those natural gas wells?"

A mocking expression crossed the baron's face. He bragged that one of his men had found the gas deposit by accident. Now the baron was scheming to buy the land at a ridiculously low price.

"Meantime," he added gloatingly, "I have a pipe down there with a valve on it. When we light the gas at night, it scares the devil out of people around here—keeps 'em from snooping."

Joe queried him about the explosion the boys had heard after seeing Rosy. The baron smirked. "That was because of faulty ignition." He went on to say that the new county road would bring too much traffic near the gang's unique hiding place in the spiral bridge. He was determined that the road construction would not be completed until he had secured the land for the gas deposit.

The boys learned from the baron how Willy Teeple had been forced to work for the gang. "I just remind Willy that if he squeals on us, his father will get the same treatment as Fenton Hardy."

The baron went on to describe the detectives' capture. He had been waylaid by several of the gang near the gas well, where his scorched briefcase had been found later by the baron.

"After that everything was simple," Prince said smugly. "We put Hardy in our special dungeon here. Foolishly he tried to break loose but we—er—discouraged him."

Joe clenched his fists. "He still managed to escape from you rats!"

"He must have pulled a Houdini act." The baron shrugged. "But he's through as a detective."

"Baron," Joe said, "you should give up. You're a two-time loser. Next time you'll go to prison for life."

"There won't be any next time," said the baron. "By the way, I intend to spring Monk Smith after we take care of you kids!"

The other men guffawed. "We'll bury the evidence, won't we, Baron?" one said with a meaningful look at the captives.

At that moment, Frank Hardy was busy eluding the two henchmen, Pete and Ferd. He had seen them emerge from the boulder entrance, and surmised that Joe and Chet were in the hands of the criminals. Frank had quickly hit upon a plan.

As the two men ranged farther from the bridge, Frank crept up to the camouflaged jeep. On the floor he found a toolbox and took out a stout screw driver and a small sledge hammer. Next he opened the hood and, groping in the darkness, finally managed to jump the wires to the ignition. The engine turned over and chugged to life.

Carrying the tools, Frank scrambled with desperate speed on to the top of the stone bridge directly over the hole underneath. He found a small fissure into which he inserted the screw driver, and tamped it as quietly as he could into the soft limestone rock.

Then the young sleuth tied one end of the nylon rope around the makeshift piton. The other end he secured tightly to his belt.

"This is my only chance," Frank thought, his heart pounding.

He grasped the rope tightly and let himself down towards the underside of the arch. Now came the crucial moment. He pushed hard against the rock with his feet, at the same time paying out ten feet of rope. The result produced a pendulum motion.

Swinging back and forth, Frank aimed for the hole. Could he make it? Twice his feet missed the opening by inches. On the third try Frank succeeded, and with a jack-knife movement, pulled himself up into the bridge.

Exhausted, Frank flopped on to the stony floor. But a moment later he untied the rope from his belt and weighted the end with a heavy stone. Frank set forth through the passageway, dimly lighted by paraffin lanterns on the wall.

Although his main concern was whether or not his decoy trick with the jeep would work, Frank noted the spiral shape of the corridor. The helix sign flashed through his mind just as a voice echoed hoarsely down the passage. "Hey, the jeep's runnin'!" someone yelled.

Frank crouched in a deep rocky niche and heard

heavy footsteps pounding on the stone floor. When he was certain the men had gone outside, Frank proceeded until he came to a side chamber hollowed from the rock. Inside he saw Chet and Joe.

"Frank!" Joe exclaimed. "How'd you get here—what—"

"Tell you later. Hurry!"

Their arms still bound to their sides, Chet and Joe followed Frank to the hole in the bridge. Frank whipped out his knife, cut their bonds and whispered. "The fireworks should start any minute. When they do, we'll slide down the rope and drop into the stream."

No sooner had he spoken than a volley of shots filled the air. "They're firing at the jeep. They think someone's trying to steal it. Come on!"

Chet was first down the rope, Joe next, then Frank. They slipped into the stream and swam quickly to cover on the far bank. They could see flashlights winking on and off in the woods like fireflies, and then, abruptly, the gunfire ceased.

The silence that ensued was almost uncanny. Cautiously the Hardys and Chet crept from concealment towards the flickering lights. The scene that met their eyes made them gasp in amazed relief and joy.

Held at bay by a force of law officers, mostly State Police, were the baron's men! Accompanying the police were Tony, Willy Teeple, and Robert Angan, the foreman.

"The baron got away—disappeared!" Tony shouted upon seeing his three pals.

Frank pointed to the stone bridge. "He's probably inside."

A tear-gas bomb was lobbed through the hole. Soon

the baron, choking and begging for mercy, staggered into view.

The Hardys and their pals clapped one another on the back and exchanged stories. "Tony, how did you and the posse find this hideout?" asked Frank.

"I just couldn't stay put when I suspected you fellows were in danger. Besides, I feel okay now." Tony explained that he had spotted Willy Teeple in town and pleaded with him, for the Hardys' sakes, to reveal what he knew about the gang. The two boys then had persuaded the Boonton police to round up a search force.

First, the lawmen had gone to the road construction site, where members of the gang, including Bond Deemer, were placed under arrest.

"We got here just in time to hear the shooting," Tony said.

Standing among the captured gangsters was the bellman from the Eagle Hotel. He readily admitted eavesdropping on the boys and hitting Tony. The Hardys and Chet related to the police what the baron had told them of his activities. Lieutenant Murphy stepped forward and praised the boys for their clever sleuthing.

"You've made a big catch," he added, indicating the baron. "That's really Gerald Thurston, master of disguises! He was the 'cousin' who had visited Yancy in the hospital."

Joe whistled. "I'll say! Intern, housebreaker, and tramp!"

Thurston glared balefully at the Hardys but said nothing. Frank, Joe, Chet, and Tony were also congratulated by Angan. "The road crew owes you a lot," he said gratefully, and Willy agreed vigorously.

The next day the boys flew back to Bayport. When Frank and Joe reached home they found their father resting in his room.

"Dad!" said Joe. "It's great to see you looking better!"

"Terrific job, fellows!" Mr Hardy said.

Frank beamed. "Thanks. I'm glad we could solve the case for you. But we're still puzzled about a few things."

The boys took seats near Mr Hardy's bed and the detective told his story. Before setting out for Kentucky, he had pulled two cards and dossiers from his files, Matlack's and Thurston's. When the baron had found Mr Hardy's briefcase, he discovered the records inside. He had promptly flown to Bayport, gone to Radley's home and stolen Matlack's card, knowing that Frank and Joe would check their father's duplicate file. Mr Hardy smiled at his sons.

"When your pursuit of Matlack ended in the grave-yard," he said, "Thurston figured you'd be discouraged and give up the case."

"Hey!" exclaimed Frank. "Now I get it!" He hurried into his fathers' study and opened the files to the Ts. Thurston's card was gone, and there was a memorandum saying, "I suspect Matlack or Thurston but because o his method I think Thurston is our man."

Frank burst into his father's room, waving the card. "Dad, what a terrific deduction!"

Mr Hardy explained that Thurston had written him threatening letters while in prison. "When he was released, I suspected he'd make trouble for me if he ever had a chance."

"He sure did!" Joe said grimly.

Frank asked how his father had escaped from the dungeon in the spiral bridge.

"Willy Teeple helped me at great risk to himself," said the detective. "One day the gang left Willy as lookout at the bridge. He unlocked my handcuffs and assisted me to the road, where Mr Teeple gave me a ride to Boonton. Willy put the handcuffs on again so that the baron would not suspect him of defecting."

Frank and Joe, pleased that the mystery was solved, wondered if another as exciting would come their way. They were soon to find out when faced with the challenging *Clue of the Screeching Owl*.

At this point, footsteps were heard on the stairs and into the room trooped Mr Prito with Tony, Chet, Biff, and Phil

Everyone cheered when Mr Prito announced that since the Kentucky wilderness would be opened up by the completion of his road project, plans had been made to develop the natural bridge as a main tourist attraction of the proposed park.

Joe grinned. "You still going to open up a hot-dog stand down there, Chet?"

The chunky boy groaned. "No more spiral bridges for me. I'm going to stick to something safe, like shot-putting!"

From Alfred Hitchcock,

Master of Mystery and Suspense—

A thrilling series of detection and adventure. Meet The Three Investigators – Jupiter Jones, Peter Crenshaw and Bob Andrews. Their motto, "We Investigate Anything", leads the boys into some extraordinary situations – even Jupiter's formidable brain-power is sometimes stumped by the bizarre crimes and weird villains they encounter. But with the occasional piece of advice from The Master himself, The Three Investigators solve a whole lot of sensational mysteries.

Armada

Armada Science Fiction

Step into the strange world of Tomorrow with Armada's exciting science fiction series.

ARMADA SCI-FI 1
ARMADA SCI-FI 2
ARMADA SCI-FI 3
ARMADA SF 4

Edited by Richard Davis

Four spinechilling collections of thrilling tales of fantasy and adventure, specially written for Armada readers.

Read about . . . The monstrous Aliens at the bottom of the garden . . . A jungle planet inhabited by huge jellies . . . A robot with a human heart . . . The terrible, terrifying Trodes . . . A mad scientist and his captive space creatures . . . The deadly rainbow stones of Lapida . . . The last tyrannosaur on earth . . . and many more.
Stories to thrill you, stories to amuse you—and stories to give you those sneaking shivers of doubt . . .

Begin your sci-fi library soon!

Armada

CAPTAIN ARMADA

has a whole shipload of exciting books for you

Armadas are chosen by children all over the world. They're designed to fit your pocket, and your pocket money too. They're colourful, gay, and there are hundreds of titles to choose from. Armada has something for everyone:

Mystery and adventure series to collect, with favourite characters and authors – like Alfred Hitchcock and The Three Investigators. The Hardy Boys. Young detective Nancy Drew. The intrepid Lone Piners. Biggles. The rascally William – and others.

Hair-raising spinechillers – ghost, monster and science fiction stories. Super craft books. Fascinating quiz and puzzle books. Lots of hilarious fun books. Many famous children's stories. Thrilling pony adventures. Popular school stories – and many more exciting titles which will all look wonderful on your bookshelf.

You can build up your own Armada collection – and new Armadas are published every month, so look out for the latest additions to the Captain's cargo.

If you'd like a complete, up-to-date list of Armada books, send a stamped, self-addressed envelope to:

Armada Books,
14 St James's Place,
London SW1A 1PS